A Medley of Short Stories

Donald F. Megnin

Copyright © 2021 by Donald F. Megnin

All rights reserved. No part of this publication may be reproduced, distributed, or transmitted in any form or by any means, including photocopying, recording, or other electronic or mechanical methods, without the prior written permission of the publisher, except in the case brief quotations embodied in critical reviews and other noncommercial uses permitted by copyright law.

ISBN: 978-1-954341-54-8 (Paperback)

The views expressed in this book are solely those of the author and do not necessarily reflect the views of the publisher, and the publisher hereby disclaims any responsibility for them.

Writers' Branding
1800-608-6550
www.writersbranding.com
orders@writersbranding.com

Contents

An Apologia ix

I. Religion 1
   A. Introduction—A Precocious Boy Becomes a Man . . . 1
   B. A Tragic Beginning, But a Brilliant Turn of Events . . . 3
   C. Forming a Group of Followers 15
   D. Jesus's Messages, Such as People Had
      Never Heard Before 20
   E. Professional Jealousy 23
   F. Arrival in Jerusalem 25
   G. The End of the Jesus of History and the Beginning of
      the Christ of Faith 29
   H. Conclusions 34
II. Experience 37
   A. An Unfortunate Beginning 37
   B. The Consequences of Experience—Part I 53
   C. The Consequences of Experience—Part II 59
   D. The Consequences of Experience—Part III 66
   E. An Unsatisfied Woman 76
   F. Wanting What Wasn't Possible 82
   G. Why Young Boys Get Excited 86
   H. Use What You Have 88
III. Farming Stories 90
   A. A Herd of Goats 90
   B. Helper 95
   C. The Elm Tree 100
   D. The Dangers of Giving Birth Alone 103
   E. A New Bicycle 105
   F. The Auction 108
   G. When Generations Clash 115
IV. Growing Up 118
   A. A Playground "Accident" 118

  B. Converting Words into Numbers.................124
  C. Equal Opportunity............................127
  D. And He Thought He Was the Father!............129
  E. A Night to Remember 131
  F. And the Neighbors Never Knew.................133
V. Ultimate Influences..................................135
  A. A Premature Judgment 135
  B. The Importance of Words and Examples 138
  C. The Man Who Made It Possible.................149
  D. Words of Wisdom 151

FOREWORD

These short stories are meant to encourage persons to examine closely what Is being taught, what they may find In their environment, and what they may carry with them for the rest of their lives as the scars, experiences and life-long influences which they will always carry with them. The stories represent not only history, but humor, tragedy, irony and lessons of what influences persons to become who and what they are. Are we aware of what is going on around us? Or are we oblivious to the subtle influences which have helped to chart our lives and which we seem not to be able to acknowledge because of indoctrination, unfortunate experiences, or a desire to escape from the daily realities of life?

The short stories carry not only illustrations of growing up, but of the experiences of living and working on a farm with little by way of creature comforts or financial security. Fortunately, short stories are meant not only to edify, but to enlighten and enthrall wherever possible, the outlook of the reader to focus upon his/her life with appreciation, humor and resignation that life has its own surprises and benefits of which we may not be aware until years later.

PREFACE

It was as an undergraduate student at Syracuse University that I was first exposed to an English course entitled The Short Story and taught by one of my favorite professors, Norman Whitney. We had to write a short story each week for the entire semester. Occasionally, he read some of them to our class as examples of what he thought were well done and could be used for our edification. He even read a couple of mine. There is nothing like having your professor read out loud what one of his students has written to give that student a source of satisfaction and commendation for what he has written.

These short stories are really a compendium of various types of impressions, experiences and thoughts which have been germinating in my mind for several years. I have long been impressed by those thinkers who questioned the views, practices and mythologies which we seem to carry with us in our daily lives and take for granted 'that's the way it is not knowing that the ancient writers composed stories which were semi-truthful accounts embellished by wishful thinking, hearsay and a mixture of mythologies meant to keep the illiterate masses subservient to their ruling religious and political masters current in those eras. Without the literacy, education and the ability to discern fact from fiction or knowledge from wishful thinking, the origins of all religions have been colorfully conveyed throughout history. What is even more surprising (disappointing) is the currency given to these beliefs and practices as if they were a real part of each person's beliefs and life. Religious fundamentalism is the outcome of years of indoctrination and the inculcation of dogma, mythology and illusory beliefs which, unfortunately, have had a devastating impact upon Hindus, Jews, Buddhists, Christians and Moslems for generations.

An Apologia

Not having written short stories since my college English classes, what follows is a series of such stories long thought about but never put into words for fear they might antagonize family, friends, fellow "seekers for truth," or persons who might object to any deviancy from what has been tradition, religious observance, or the absolute acceptance of authority as written and taught throughout the centuries. When I read the stories of how the current Pope Benedict XVI has tried to absolve himself from not having taken the responsibility of separating bishops and priests who were the instigators of sexual exploitation of children while in charge of their parishes when he was a cardinal, the question of authority became a very pungent and important issue for those of us who have served in parishes as ministers.

First, the question of authority is and has been a crucial issue for those of us who seek truth before belief, honesty before the protection of status, justice before self-serving excuses, integrity before convenience, the application of scientific testing of long-held suppositions, in place of respect for persons simply because they hold highly placed positions, and applying reason to each and every role played by individuals whether by tradition, election, or illegal seizure of power.

Second, the history of humankind has been irregular at best and blatantly exploitative at worst depending upon which individuals or authorities were in power. It has taken thousands of years for human beings to recognize their limitations and the impact that such limitations can have upon them. Even today, we still find religious authorities who take for granted their infallibility simply by virtue of the status assigned to them. It is incredible that the pope still believes his priests, nuns, bishops, and himself should remain celibate because an earlier pope wished to cleanse the Catholic Church of nepotism. Their sons thought they should succeed their papal fathers as princes followed their father kings in natural succession. It is the consideration of this author that had the pope renounced celibacy both for himself and his religious cohorts, there would not be such a dearth of clergy to fill the millions of parishes around the world. The caveat, however, is such persons would still wish to perpetuate the prevailing myths and untestable beliefs that are the mainstays of their religion.

Third, the beginning of every religion (Hinduism, Buddhism, Confucianism, Taoism, Judaism, Christianity, Islam, Sikhism, Mormonism) were started by persons of high status simply stating to the uneducated, illiterate, and subservient masses what they have written is the "Word of God," the founder of their religious tradition, or exploiting their status as a means of the self-perpetuation of themselves, their offsprings, or families for perpetuity. The positions assigned and occupied by the "leaders of the faithful" were devised, staffed, and assumed to be their right as the most educated, wealthiest, and/or powerful in their respective communities of faith. If anyone should challenge these individuals who had designated themselves these high positions or were appointed to these positions of authority, such a person was soon exiled, imprisoned, or killed depending upon the leniency of the most powerful authorities of their day.

Fourth, what follows in this first short story is an attempt to clarify and remove the traditional gloss and mythological components of the "Christian faith." Why anyone would want to embellish a truly remarkable, logical, and tragic beginning of the life of Jesus into a series of myths, legends, and incomprehensible beliefs is astounding to this writer. What "religious authorities" have done is to create a mythological religion based on figments of their imaginations and need to justify themselves by linking their beliefs with a host of symbols of a God "up there in heaven," a God who is "ever present," a God who was "revealed in a man," a God who welcomes us to heaven "upon our deaths." And what is even more incredible, men, women, and children died for such a belief system that was taught them as the absolute truth without which their lives would be wasted and consigned to another figure known as Satan and hell, another part of the myth, should they not believe what was being taught to them!

With these caveats in mind, the following story may make more sense and allow you to consider who and what Jesus of Nazareth was and the meaning his life may have tried to illustrate apart from the fantasy that ancient authorities have tried to impose upon who he was and what he tried to do.

I.

Religion

A. Introduction—A Precocious Boy Becomes a Man

In looking back upon the early days of the development of the Christian faith, we should not forget the vast majority of people of this era were part of the huge, illiterate, and unwashed masses who believed in religious fantasy and mythology. These early peoples who became members of the Christian religion had neither the education nor the means by which to evaluate what was being told to them (a condition that was universal among the followers of all religions). They could not become knowledgeable and discerning members of the human community in the context by which we would evaluate discerning, enlightened, educated peoples of the twenty-first century. The leadership of government, religion, enterprise, and economic activities was controlled by less than 1 percent of the population of those times. The vast, illiterate, and uninformed masses were easily led to believe whatever the leaders of their tribes, countries, and religion told them. They had no way of evaluating what was being communicated to them and what was expected of them or even question what was told to them about governance, religion, the universe, or the *how* and *why* the activities of men or of nature were structured. The masses only knew what they were told by the people in positions of authority and power. It was assumed by the mass illiterates that those in power should know better than anyone else what was expected of them: to work, to accept, to follow, and to believe what was told to them! The interpretation of the world and belief systems were handed down to the commoners to accept what was being said to them by persons in positions of authority and power. There was no way in which even educated persons of these ancient times could evaluate what was real and what was fantasy. Even today, we find certain religious authorities who claim special powers (knowledge) based, not on their brilliance of intellect, but upon the traditional basis of power: tradition!

Subsequently, in retelling the story of Jesus from a nontraditional point of view, the reader should remember this is an interpretation that is different, yet plausible, and at odds with the familiar mythical origins of Christianity that have long been taught to generations of children over the past two thousand years of its creation and continuity. What I am suggesting is that we remember the time period of this ancient story and recognize that the intellectual frame of reference of the twenty-first century is different, critical, and vastly more erudite in applying sources of information from an enormously expanded universe of knowledge that ancient peoples neither had nor even knew existed.

B. A Tragic Beginning, But a Brilliant Turn of Events

The Roman army base was just outside the village of Nazareth. The girls and young women were constantly warned by their parents to be careful going from their village to the next.

"Stay on the main road, Mary. Don't use the shortcut across the fields to the path leading to Zophia. The Roman soldiers are nearby and they have been known to seize young girls," her mother told her.

"I'll be all right, Mother. A group of us girls are going over to visit Elizabeth this afternoon. We'll stay on the main road," Mary promised.

Mary's mother wasn't so sure. Just last week, their neighbor's twenty-year-old daughter had been taken into "custody," as the Romans called it. She was raped repeatedly by the nine-men squad that had found her walking along the road behind their encampment. It was common knowledge among the Nazarenes that the Romans couldn't be trusted.

The shortest way to Mary's friend was just behind the barricade separating the Roman garrison from the outskirts of Nazareth. Mary wanted to take some of her friends with her but only Ruth was able to go.

Surely, the Romans wouldn't try to stop them as they would make their way past the garrison, Mary thought.

What Mary did not know was that the troops had been issued their weekly wineskins with which to satisfy themselves over the weekend. The soldiers were on duty six days a week. Their day off was usually spent drinking themselves into a stupor if they could not find eligible courtesans waiting outside their compound. The soldiers were fed up with the repeated tryst with these women. Most of the soldiers were far from their families. They could only bring them to Judea if they promised to settle down in this Roman colony. Since most of the soldiers were reluctant to stay more than their two-year requirement overseas, they had two options facing them each weekend: one, to drink themselves into oblivion and sleep the entire weekend or, two, to make use of the numerous women waiting outside the garrison gates with whom they could find some physical pleasure at very little cost to themselves. Far better was the chance encounter with one of the girls living nearby.

As Mary and Ruth made their way past the perimeter of the Roman compound, two of the soldiers saw them. They agreed that if they could catch the girls, each would have one for himself. The two girls were hurrying past the gates. The two Roman soldiers ran after them and caught them. They forced them to come into the valley below the cantonment where a few bushes hid them from the sight of any passersby. The two teenage girls were raped repeatedly after the soldiers bound their mouths with course pieces of their tunics that they took off.

After two hours, the soldiers let the girls go on their way. One of the soldiers spoke a few words of Aramaic and warned them, "Don't say anything to anyone about what happened to you. You know what the custom is. Your family will disown you if you tell them what happened, and you'll be subjected to a stoning for what you did!"

The girls remained silent. As they continued on their way to Zophia, Mary said, "I'm going to tell my mother. She'll know it wasn't our fault."

"I will too," Ruth said. "We better not tell Elizabeth what happened to us.

The fewer people that know, the better it'll be." They both agreed.

They returned to Nazareth by way of the valley around Cheulloth. It was the long way home but one that skirted the Roman cantonment entirely. They weren't likely to encounter any soldiers on this route.

Upon reaching home, Mary told her mother she wasn't feeling well.

"Did you have something to drink at Elizabeth's home?" her mother asked. "Only a cup of water."

"What happened to your cloak, Mary? There are blood spots on it!"

"Mother, I don't know how to say this, but Ruth and I were raped by two Roman soldiers from the nearby cantonment."

"Oh, you poor girls! If I thought it would do any good, I'd go to the Roman legion office and complain about what happened to you! But if I do that, your future as a wife would be in jeopardy! I'm sorry, Mary, but you'll have to stay home from now on. We can't take a chance on a future husband of yours not being interested in you as his wife because you've been raped! You'll have to stay with me here in the house until we find out if you're pregnant or not! If you are, then the chances of your finding a husband are next to nil. No man wants a used woman for a wife!"

Mary started crying. There was nothing she could do. She had not encouraged the rape. She and her friend were the victims of the brutality of the Roman occupation forces. The Romans couldn't care less. It was necessary to hold these people down as one Jewish compliant king after another did the Romans' bidding.

As the days stretched into months, it became more and more obvious that Mary was pregnant.

"Mother, what am I going to do? No man will want me for a wife! It wasn't my fault what the Roman soldier did to me!" she said as she started crying again.

"There is one man who recently asked about you, Mary. He said he hadn't seen you in some time and wondered if you were ill. I told him the whole tragic story because he seemed so interested in what had become of you."

"Who is he, Mother? Do you think he might marry me even as I am?"

"His name is Joseph from the House of David. He lives just around the corner. He's a carpenter with a very good business. He lost his wife two years ago and has been interested in you. He wanted to know what had happened to you. I told him the whole story about how you were raped. He felt genuinely sorry for you. He said if you ever wanted to get married, he's available. You couldn't ask for a better man than he, Mary."

"He's at least twenty years older than I am, Mother. Do you really think he would marry me?"

"That's what he said. In your condition, I don't think there would be anyone else available. We certainly don't want to tell anyone at the temple what happened to you! They might want to carry out the ritual of a stoning! If you're interested, I'll talk to Joseph tomorrow."

Mary's mother went to visit their neighbor around the corner that next day.

He was just getting ready to open his shop when she came in the door. "Ah, Mary's mother. How are you today?"

"I'm fine. I just wanted to talk to you if you're still interested in marrying my daughter."

"It's strange that you should ask. I had a dream last night about your daughter. It was as if someone told me to go ahead and marry her. She will be a very good wife and mother, I dreamed. Since she's near the time of giving birth, I thought I'd marry her and give the child a name so that it won't be viewed as one of those bastards whose lives are so tragic because of the abuse they suffer."

"Oh, would you really do that, Mr. Joseph? It would be a real blessing to my daughter and the child, if she could become your wife!"

"Yes. I'll talk to the rabbi this afternoon and tell him we'd like to plan for a wedding this coming Sunday. It shouldn't be a problem. He's a very understanding man."

"Thank you very much, Mr. Joseph. I'm sure my daughter will be greatly relieved and pleased to become your wife! The baby needs a father and a mother. It wasn't my daughter's fault that she was raped!"

After work that afternoon, Joseph went to see the rabbi. The rabbi had just completed his afternoon readings and prayers.

"Rabbi Solomon, I'd like to request your service in order to marry the girl who lives around the corner from me. You know the one, also from the David family."

"How long have you known the family?"

"They've lived near me for many years. The father died this past year, but his daughter, Mary, is a young girl of sixteen. I've always been impressed with her. She smiles so easily and is very friendly each time I've gone past their house."

"Hasn't she put on a lot of weight recently? I've only seen her off and on, but I remember her as a very beautiful young girl when I conducted her father's funeral."

"Yes, she has put on considerable weight, but that's all right with me. My former wife was also rather plump, as you will recall."

On that next Sunday morning, Joseph and Mary were married. Joseph, in keeping with his dream, refrained from copulating with Mary until after the birth of her child. It was only a little over a month before she gave birth. Mary had moved into Joseph's house and began taking over the household chores even as pregnant as she was. Her mother helped clean and taught Mary how to cook the lamb stew that Joseph liked so, so much.

Since the Romans issued an order that all expectant parents were to go to Bethlehem to register their newborns, Joseph and Mary left Nazareth to go to Bethlehem to comply with the Roman requirement. It was in that city that Mary's baby was born. Joseph assisted Mary in delivering the baby boy. They had tried to stay in the local inn, but it was full. The owner suggested he could put them up for the night in his barn behind the inn. They had taken him up on his offer, and the little boy was born in the barn.

After Mary fed the baby and slept for a while, she asked Joseph, "What should we call him, Joseph?"

As was traditional in the Jewish household, the father designated what his son should be called.

"Since I'm going to look upon him as my son, Mary, why don't we call him Jesus from the lineage of the House of David, which is also my family's background. That way, no one will ever know the real story of how you became pregnant. Everyone will assume he's my son."

"Oh thank you, Joseph! He's such a sweet little boy. He hasn't really cried much since he was born. I'm sure he'll grow up to be just like you!"

Joseph, Mary, and the baby stayed in Bethlehem for a few more days. The Jewish king had issued an order that all male children should be put to death since they might become king and challenge his authority and that of his family. Joseph, Mary, and Jesus continued on to Egypt until they got word that the edict had been rescinded by the Jewish king.

Mary, Joseph, and the baby returned to Joseph's house and workshop in Nazareth. It had been many years since a baby was in the Joseph household. Most of Joseph's sons and daughters, by his first marriage, had grown up and moved away to other villages nearby. Mary took very good care of her newborn son. Joseph spent more of his time in his workshop or helping his neighbors build their houses. Since he was a carpenter, his services were in great demand, even though he wanted to spend more time in the household watching the baby grow from day to day.

As time went on, Mary and Joseph had other children: James, John, and Mark were the boys; and Elizabeth, Mary, and Seleena were the girls. When Jesus was twelve, Joseph and Mary went to the temple in Jerusalem to pray during the feast of the Passover. This was one of the Jewish high holy days, and all pious Jews wished to attend the temple in Jerusalem. It was only after they had returned home that Mary and Joseph discovered Jesus was not with them. They returned to the temple and found him holding forth in a discussion with the temple elders. Not only were Joseph and Mary shocked but they were also downright angry.

"Why didn't you tell us where you were going? We've been looking all over for you! Your brothers and sisters didn't even know where you were!"

"I'm sorry. I should have told you. I wanted to hear what the elders had to say about how people should live and how they should get along with each other."

"Well, don't forget you're only twelve years old. You've just had your bar mitzvah. If you had questions about religion, you should have asked the elders those questions then!"

One of the elders spoke up, "On behalf of my colleagues and myself, I should like to suggest that you and your husband enroll your son in the rabbinic school in Nazareth. The questions he has asked and the discussions he has conducted with us suggest he has a great future ahead of him as a fellow rabbi. We do not recommend such a change in direction of any youngster whom we have seen here before, but he is such an unusually intelligent boy. We felt we should tell you what he should be prepared to do with his life."

Needless to say, this was a shock to Mary and Joseph. They had expected him to follow in Joseph's footsteps and become a carpenter. As they returned to Nazareth, they had a long discussion of what they should do.

"Do you really think Jesus should go to school, Joseph? None of the other children around us have had this opportunity."

"But if the elders in Jerusalem have said this is what we should do, Mary, I think we should send him to school. I'm making a very fine income and have saved a considerable amount of shekels in my lifetime. We can afford to send him to school."

And so Jesus attended the rabbinic school where he learned not only how to read and write but was also taught the scriptures and the history of the Jewish people. What his neighbors didn't know was that he very likely also taught his younger brothers and sisters how to read and write while working for the next eighteen years in Joseph's workshop.

Jesus was a very diligent and hardworking member of Joseph's family. He worked daily with his father and brothers after school. Joseph often took him along when he went to help build the inside of the mud-baked homes of their neighbors after the outside construction had dried.

As the years went by, since Jesus was the oldest of the boys, his father put him in charge when he was unable to supervise the construction himself. It gave Jesus a rare opportunity to become familiar with other people, often giving them directions of what they should do and how to do their work. He also enjoyed the seniority of being "the person in charge" from day to day. Joseph increasingly gave him the assignments of where to go, what to do, and Jesus let him know when the jobs were completed. He gained an enormous amount of confidence in his own ability to think through the problems and issues confronting them in their daily work assignments.

Mary was pleased with her eldest son. She gradually forgot the cruel way in which his life had been conceived. She was ever grateful and thankful to Joseph for having accepted her in spite of being raped and impregnated by the Roman soldier. His origin was never questioned by his siblings or neighbors. They simply accepted as fact that he was born before they were and, hence, was the eldest brother. The neighbors, who might have wondered about his unusual early birth shortly after Joseph had married Mary, never questioned that he was the son of Joseph. They thought miracles happen. Jesus must have been one of those miracles of which they had always been taught to believe. Therefore, he was one of those rare and unusual cases of an "earlier birth" than normal. Because he grew into such a good, intelligent, hardworking, and caring individual, they never thought anymore about his birth.

Jesus began to experience the fact that his neighbors and friends came to him for advice about what they should do in a variety of cases in which they faced dilemmas.

A young man came into the shop one day and asked Jesus what he should do about the problem he was having with his father over his inheritance. "Jesus, I'm twenty years old, and I want to travel to other parts of the world before I get married and settle down. The Roman Empire is vast, and I'd like to see some of it before I have to stay in one place for the rest of my life. I've talked to my father, and he wants me to stay and help my brother on the farm. But I want to do something else with my life. If I don't see what's out there now, I won't know what I should eventually do!"

"Do you have the money to travel and find your way in places where the people have a different way of life and may not speak your language?"

"I've asked my father for my share of the inheritance which my brother and I will receive. He's agreed to give it to me even though he'd like to have me stay and help on the farm."

"Well, I wish you all the best. But don't forget it's not going to be easy for you among people whom you do not know. What do you think will happen if you don't like what you see and experience somewhere else?"

"I guess I'd want to return home." "Would you be welcomed?"

"I'm sure my father would accept my return. My older brother has already told our father not to give me my share of the inheritance. He said I should stay home and help him on the farm."

The young man went off to faraway places. Jesus witnessed what he had predicted. In two years' time, the young man returned and asked for forgiveness from his father. Fortunately for the young man, his father took him in again even though his older brother greatly resented his return!

Whenever a neighbor had a problem, he came over to the shop to talk with Jesus. The word went out that he was a very good listener and gave good advice. Joseph recognized that Jesus had an unusual talent of listening quietly to a person seeking advice. At times, it was inconvenient because of the pressure to complete a job for a neighbor, but as the brothers of Jesus matured, they slowly took over more and more of the responsibilities of helping their father.

Joseph would counsel them with the comment, "Jesus is actually doing us a great service by listening to the problems of our neighbors. They come into our shop and see what we're doing. If they need a bed or a stool or a new roof, they come to us first. That's a big help to us. He's an excellent carpenter, but he's even better than the rabbi because he listens to the problems people have before telling them what they should do. The rabbi, on the other hand, tells people what they have to do and pays no attention to what they've said or asked."

John, a cousin of Jesus, who was a preacher, stopped by one day and told Jesus, "Look, if you're such a good listener and advisor to people, you ought to join me in preaching to them what they should do to improve their lives. Why don't you come down to the river tomorrow and let me baptize you so that you'll become qualified to counsel people and help them overcome their difficulties? Your father tells me he's amazed at how often and how many people come to ask you for advice. I think you ought to join me in preaching the word of what people should do with their lives and how they should live.

The way people behave these days is about as far from how they ought to live as you can imagine! With your talent, you'd be a natural preacher in the service of our God."

After hearing John's advice, Jesus went down to the river that next afternoon.

John was pleased to see him.

"I'm glad you've finally made up your mind, Jesus. There are too few of us who are concerned with how people live and behave toward one another. You've got a great future ahead of you."

"What you're suggesting is really what I've been thinking about, John, for some time. Ever since Joseph died, I've felt I should be doing something else with my life. I enjoy my contact with other people very much. They seem to listen to me when they ask for my advice. I don't think I can do as much for others if I stay in the workshop. That's why I've come today. James and John can take care of the business. They're old enough and have learned from our father how to become expert carpenters. I'm going to take your suggestion, and after you baptize me, I'm going to go off into the wilderness for a few weeks and test what I can and cannot do."

John took Jesus into the water with him. "Jesus, I baptize you with this water which has sprung from the distant mountains. Even as we know not from whence it has come, so too do we not know where the future will take us. May this water represent the beginning of a new life which you are about to undertake in the service of mankind. May you become the man you were meant to be."

Jesus felt much better. Since he had never taken a bath in the river before, he felt cleansed and like a new person. He appreciated John's words saying the water represented a cleansing from the old life and the beginning of a new one. *I'm going off to see what life is like*, he told himself, *in the solitude and silence of the wilderness.*

He returned home and told his mother where he was going and what he planned to do. "Mother, I've got to take some time off and think through what I really want to do with my life. You and Joseph have been very good to us children. My brothers and sisters are now grown-up and have their own lives to lead. I'm not sure what I'm going to do yet, but I'd like to go off into the wilderness and see if I can figure out what I should do with my life."

"John has really gotten to you, hasn't he? He's the one who suggested you should be working with people instead of working in your father's carpenter shop, isn't he? You do have a way with people, Jesus. They seem to come to you whenever they have any problems and ask you for advice. I can see you should be someone who works with people and helps them solve their problems. I'll pack you some food to take with you. If you stay in the wilderness too long, you'll starve to death. Don't forget to come back when you've run out of enough food to eat!"

Jesus laughed. "You don't think I can survive on my own, do you, Mother?"

"I know you young men all think you can survive anywhere. I'm only saying, don't forget to come back after your desert foray. You won't find many people out in the wilderness. They're all living in the towns and villages of Judea."

Mary packed dried meat, bread, and water for Jesus to take with him in two leather pouches. "This should be enough for you at least for a couple of weeks, maybe even longer, Jesus. Do be careful of the wild animals that are out there. Be sure to take your father's staff with you for protection."

"Thanks, Mother. I'll be all right. I'll be back after I've settled some personal issues about what I'm going to do with the rest of my life."

Jesus set off for his "forty days in the wilderness." He wasn't sure where he was going. He thought he'd head for the mountains first. He liked the view of the landscape from a good vantage point. He felt it helped him to see himself as a part of the fragments that composed the world. Too many people think they are the be-all and end-all of life, when we're only a small part of creation. We can see, think, feel, and act independently when we're alone and free from the constant contact with our fellow human beings. He ate and drank sparingly at first, but then found a spring that came from out of the rocks on the mountainside. He found a flat area near the top of the mountain and decided there he would stay. He spent time in prayer that he had learned in the school and synagogue. His parents had encouraged him to go to the temple as often as possible while still a boy. Since the elders recognized there was something special about him when he spent those three days talking with them at age twelve, he had learned all that he could in the rabbinic school. He was glad the elders had encouraged Joseph and Mary to send him to school to learn how to read and write and the tenets of Judaism. He recalled what the elders had said to Mary and Joseph, "Any young boy who can ask such good questions and respond to the words of us elders deserves to become educated!"

Subsequently, Jesus became one of the few educated young boys in Nazareth who wasn't the son of a rabbi or of a village elder. When his brothers wanted to go to the school, Joseph and Mary were told, "Have your sons learn your trade, Joseph. We need good carpenters. It's only the few brilliant boys who can keep up with the teaching of the elders."

Unbeknown to them, Jesus taught his brothers and sisters to read and write. The members of the David family were the only ones in the village whose sons and daughters could be counted among the educated. The neighbors knew nothing about their "education," but they were impressed with how they seemed to know a lot more than any of the other children as they were growing up.

What should I do? Jesus asked himself repeatedly. *I can stay and work in my father's workshop. I could open one myself since I know what a carpenter does for a living. I could get married and settle down as one of the skilled workers in the area. I'd really like to become a rabbi and help teach people how to live and work together in peace and harmony. But I've not had the benefit of long years of teaching which are required of rabbis.* Yes, he learned the rules of Judaism and all of the scriptures. *I've learned a lot of them, but I wouldn't be accepted by a congregation without that level of higher education. I could become what John is: a wandering Jewish preacher who constantly interacts with whomever he comes into contact. He hasn't had any rabbinical training either. But he seems to enjoy going from town to town telling people how to live and what they must do to be "saved." Actually, he's made a big impression on anyone whom he has met,* he told himself. *What bothers me about what he calls "his ministry" is the fact that no one seems to want to join him in his travels around the countryside. He's a "loner." He doesn't have anyone with whom to communicate when he feels the need to talk things through and decide what he should do.*

Jesus spent a few hours every day in prayer which he had learned from the elders. He felt close to what he called "God, his Father." Not that he denied Joseph as his father, but his mother had once told him, when they were alone together, he wasn't really Joseph's son. She had been raped by a Roman soldier. Jesus never forgot. He also never told anyone about his origin. Joseph was so good to him. It never had occurred to Jesus that he wasn't the personification of everything anyone would want in a father. That's why he had stayed with his family as long as he did. It was only after Joseph died that Jesus began his quest to determine what he really should do with his life. And now, finally, he had the opportunity to begin to think for himself. He no longer felt the obligation to stay with his parents, brothers, and sisters. They were now all adults and could look after themselves.

After four weeks of these thoughts, prayers, personal tests of endurance, and sorting out his future, he decided it was time to return to his village. Mary was glad to see him again. "Welcome home, Jesus. Did you run out of food and water?"

"No, Mother." He laughed. "If you look in the bags, you'll find some food leftover. I spent a lot of my time thinking, fasting, and praying. I really didn't need all of the food which you sent with me. I found a mountain spring for water so that I really didn't need anything."

"What about the wild animals? Weren't they a danger to you?"

"No. Actually, the deer became very friendly and didn't seem to mind that I used one of their mountain meadows as a place to stay. I didn't see any mountain lions. No. It was a very worthwhile and necessary period of time in which I finally have figured out what I should do with my life."

"And what is that going to be?"

"I'm going to become an advisor and counselor for my fellow human beings. They seem to want to talk to me, so this is the way in which I can contribute to their lives. They seem unable to do so for themselves. I thought maybe I'd ask a couple of my neighbors if they wanted to join me in touring Galilee to see what we could do to help people who seem incapable of helping themselves."

"So you're going to follow the path of your cousin, John? I hope you won't become as hostile and dogmatic as he is! It's really hard to believe he cares about people. He seems to condemn them more than help them with their problems!"

"He means well, Mother. He just doesn't seem to know how to relate to ordinary people. His heart's in the right place. That's why I let him baptize me. I want to relate to people this same idea of his that God should become the first priority before anything else."

C. Forming a Group of Followers

In contrast to his cousin, John, Jesus knew he had to have a group of men who would work with him in conveying his message of hope and transformational behavior. Interestingly enough, Jesus recognized he had been fortunate to have become a literate and knowledgeable person due to his parents' favorable response to the men in the temple suggesting he should be educated because of his precociousness and intelligence in his questioning them about religion. Since he had learned the basic concepts of Judaism and related easily to other persons, he had no difficulty recruiting what were called "disciples." It is still remarkable that when he saw Simon and Andrew casting a net into the Sea of Galilee, he suggested, if they followed him, he would make them "fishers of men." They did exactly what he wished and became his first followers. He then saw James and John working with their father and servants repairing their nets. They, too, left their father and work and went with Jesus. The others whom he chose were Philip, Bartholomew, Matthew, Thomas, James (the son of Alphaeus), Thaddaeus, another Simon (a Canaanite), and Judas Iscariot. With this group of men, he made his way over the next three years throughout Galilee preaching to groups of persons who were fascinated by his intellect, ideas, and individualism. If the religious followers of the faith questioned him (the Pharisees) about what he and his followers were doing, eating, or working on the Sabbath, he replied, "Have you never read what David did, when he was in need and was hungry? He, and those who were with him, entered the house of God. When Abiathar was high priest, he ate the Bread of the Presence, which was not lawful to eat, and gave it to those who were with him. The Sabbath was made for man, not man for the Sabbath, so the Son of Man is Lord even on the Sabbath."

This was just one illustration of how the religious authorities were constantly trying to find ways to trap him in contradicting the religious practices of Judaism. His favorite method of conveying religious ideas was by means of parables. One illustration was when he told of the man sowing seed. It only grew and produced food if the planter had planted the seed on fertile ground. If the seed were sown on rocky soil, or among weeds, it would produce nothing. When he was alone with his disciples, they asked him the meaning of his illustrations (parables). He told them the sower is the one who plants the word of God. The illustrations (parables) are what people must do to become religious followers of what God wishes them to do with their lives. The stories were ways to try to communicate with people who understood basic concepts by observation of things that were familiar to them. Jesus told the disciples, "Parables are what I use so that people will understand how their lives can be illustrations of the concepts I'm trying to convey. Is a lamp brought in to be put under a bushel or under a bed and not on a stand? For there is nothing hid, except to be made manifest; nor is anything secret, except to come to light."

In other words, he told his disciples, "People are to apply what they hear to their own lives. If any man has ears to hear, let him hear. Take heed what you hear; the measure you give will be the measure you get, and still more will be given to you. For to him who has will more be given; and from him who has not, even what he has will be taken away."

Jesus was calling upon his followers to change the direction of their lives even as he did. Leaving the carpentry shop and business to wander first in the wilderness and then to recruit like-minded men was to become a totally transforming friendship for those whom he recruited. Their lives would never be the same again. They left their families, their occupations, and their daily lives behind to wander with this man, whom they came to respect, trust, and believe could transform the life of anyone with whom he came in contact. The disciples became the surrogates of Jesus to do whatever he had demonstrated should be done to assist people who had little or no hope to improve their lives. They were to do what Jesus did. They were to become the agents of change in the lives of those with whom they interacted. Their goals were changed by virtue of living, traveling, and interacting with Jesus on a daily basis. When Jesus told parables, the disciples did not understand what he meant. He had to explain their meaning almost every time he used them.

Jesus explained the meaning of his parables to his followers when he was alone with them, "If I use direct speech, it would cause the religious authorities to take umbrage and wish to silence me from further disseminating ideas which would question their authority and make people think for themselves. Parables are an indirect way for me to convey my message which the authorities will view as subversive and threatening to these persons in authority or in positions of power. They wish to continue to exercise their authority over the people, illiterate masses, of our world. They cannot tolerate direct words against them for fear of what the people might do to correct the inequities between those in power and the rest us who are powerless. It is the educated elite, persons in positions of authority—governmental or religious—therefore, who find my words threatening and offensive. What I'm saying is threatening to their continued dominance and control over the masses who neither know how to read or write. If I spoke directly, rather than in parables, I would be fomenting revolt and undermining the authorities who wish to continue to rule, control, and exploit the people as they see fit. Hence, I've developed this method to communicate my message so that the authorities will not become completely antagonistic toward me."

It is remarkable that these men from the lowest ranks of their society joined the ranks of Jesus's followers. Very likely they saw no future in the trades they were following. Some of them left their wives and children to fend for themselves. With large families, however, such an additional burden was absorbed with little or no rancor. At least, there is no record of any recriminations being made by a deserted wife. The attachment of men with no economic wealth to those who were intellectually brilliant evidently seems to have been an acceptable practice even in non-Christian circles (Buddhists, Hindus, Sikhs, Greeks, and Huns). In Jesus, his followers had a daily example of a different way to interact with all manner of human beings. His disciples took their cues from observing him and how he interacted with people on all levels of society. His encounters with the Sadducees and Pharisees in which he used parables to speak with them, revealed the different levels of communication he used among the educated aristocrats which his disciples did not understand and which he had to literally translate so that they could know what he had told these men of intellect and means.

In what has been called "The Sermon on The Mount," Jesus tried to convey not only to his disciples what they should do but to the thousands who were following him about to learn, see, and do the good he was attempting to demonstrate for those who were among the outcasts of Jewish society. It was a brilliant summation of not only his life but of his message to those who wished to live different lives from what they had daily experienced. What church historians seem to have missed is this intellectual differentiation which Jesus took on to appeal to the masses of Jewish society.

He came from the working class. He was very likely one of the exceptions to his class by virtue of having been given an education unavailable to other boys of his age and social milieu. Hence, his need to "translate" to his disciples the meaning of the parables he used was because when speaking to members of the upper classes they could understand. Interestingly enough, the educated elite of Judaism rallied around him because, not only did he relate easily to them (as an educated Jew) but because he spoke to anyone who asked a question of him or asked for his assistance. Unfortunately for Jesus, by virtue of associating with the lowest class of Judaism, he was accused by his intellectual opponents as one who associated and ate with "harlots, tax collectors and sinners." Indeed, these were the very elements of society with whom these "good people" did not associate! For Jesus, there was no differentiation between the haves and the have-nots in the world he was interested in creating.

As with any of the great religious figures of history, the disciples saw in Jesus a personality whom they had never encountered before. His religious views promised a difference in their lives that likewise they had never seen or heard expressed by anyone else. Jesus represented the rare quality of demonstrating how people should interact with one another. His example made people think he could do anything to help them. All they had to do was to be touched by him, or if they should touch him in some way, they would be healed of their ailments and infirmities. His reputation became larger than life. Even a Roman centurion thought him capable of healing his daughter just by saying the word that his daughter was healed. Little wonder that Jesus became a hero and legend in the communities through which he passed.

It should not be misconstrued. Jesus felt himself to be a messenger only to the Jews. When a woman came to him to be healed, he told her since she was not Jewish, he could do nothing for her. She would have to seek help from someone else. When she said "but even the dogs eat the crumbs from under the tables of Jews," he was so impressed by her response that he said, "Your problem will be resolved."

Jesus delegated responsibilities to his disciples. Peter was placed in the position to carry on his work should anything happen to him. The others were sent in twos and threes to various villages to spread the word of Jesus's beliefs and demonstrations of the love of God for the Jews or anyone who helped another to live a life of hope and trust in the love of God. To share human experiences of love, forgiveness, and the results of efforts that produced a livelihood to be shared with others in communal consideration meant each person was a valuable member of the human community worthy of God's love and generosity. The disciples were to demonstrate these beliefs of Jesus as they traveled with him throughout Galilee.

D. Jesus's Messages, Such as People Had Never Heard Before

Part of the inimitable legacy of Jesus was his ability to address messages to a given person or to a group of persons such as they had never heard before. On one occasion, the scribes and Pharisees brought a woman who had been caught in adultery and placed her in the midst of the assembly. They said to him, "Teacher, this woman has been caught in the act of adultery. Now in the law, Moses commanded us to stone such. What do you say about her?"

Jesus bent down and wrote with his finger on the ground. They continued to ask him. He stood up and said to them, "Let him who is without sin among you be the first to throw a stone at her."

Once more, Jesus bent down and wrote with his finger on the ground. When these men heard what he had said, they went away, one by one, beginning with the eldest. Jesus was left alone with the woman standing before him. Jesus looked up and said to her, "Woman, where are they? Has no one condemned you?"

She said, "No one."

Jesus said, "Neither do I condemn you. Go and do not sin again."

Jesus was a very unique person. He turned the questions of his tormentors into questioning them concerning what they were doing so that they might learn to question their own assumptions. One of the most interesting and compelling examples he used was that of the prodigal son. Here was a young man who wished to see the world and repented when his funds ran out.

As Jesus told the story he said, "There was a man who had two sons. The younger of the two said to his father, 'Father, give to me the share of property that falls to me'. And the man divided his living between them. Not many days later, the younger son gathered all he had and took a journey into a far country, and there squandered his property in loose living. And when he had spent everything, a great famine arose in that country, and he began to be in want. So he went and joined himself to one of the citizens of that country, who sent him into his fields to feed swine. He would gladly have fed on the pods that the swine ate. No one gave him anything. When he came to himself, he said, 'How many of my father's hired servants have bread enough and to spare, while I perish here with hunger! I will arise and go to my father and I will say to him, 'Father, I have sinned against heaven and before you. I am no longer worthy to be called your son. Treat me as one of your hired servants.' He arose and came to his father. While he was yet at a distance, his father saw him and had compassion and ran and embraced him and kissed him. 'Father, I have sinned against heaven and before you. I am no longer worthy to be called your son.' But the father said to his servants, 'Bring quickly the best robe and put it on him. Put a ring on his hand and shoes on his feet and bring the fatted calf and kill it. Let us eat and be merry, for this my son was dead and is alive again. He was lost and is found.'"

Jesus demonstrated over and over again that in spite of what people do, they can overcome their disabilities and become part of the community of which they were once a part if they are truly sorry for what they have done. For Jesus, no one is beyond the pale of forgiveness, if he or she recognizes the errors they have made and are willing to start over again. Life for Jesus was one continuous journey in which to demonstrate how it can be improved by the actions of people who recognize their mistakes. Those who are among the wealthy, from Jesus's view, have their rewards. It is the people who have little or nothing that he came to offer hope and improvement for the future.

When he was criticized for helping people on the Sabbath or during the holy days of Judaism, he told the story about the woman who lost one of her coins. She hunted and hunted throughout her house for the coin that was lost until she found it. She then was so thankful she invited her neighbors to help her celebrate with a party on the Sabbath.

On another occasion, a young lawyer stood up in one of Jesus's discussions one day and asked, "Teacher, what shall I do to inherit eternal life?"

Jesus replied, "What is written in the law? How do you read?"

The young man responded, "You shall love the Lord your God with all your heart and with all your soul and with all your strength and with all your mind and your neighbor as yourself."

And Jesus said to him, "You have answered right; do this and you will live."

But the young man wanted to justify himself and said to Jesus, "And who is my neighbor?"

Jesus replied, "A man was going down from Jerusalem to Jericho, and he fell among robbers, who stripped him and beat him, and departed, leaving him half-dead. Now by chance, a priest was going down that road and, when he saw him, passed by on the other side. So likewise, a Levite, when he came to the place and saw him, passed by on the other side. But a Samaritan, as he journeyed, came to where he was and, when he saw him, had compassion and went to him and bound up his wounds, pouring on oil and wine. He then set him on his own beast and brought him to an inn and took care of him. The next day, he took out two denarii and gave them to the innkeeper saying, 'Take care of him; and whatever more you spend, I will repay you when I come back.' Which of these three do you think proved neighbor to him who fell among the robbers?"

The lawyer answered, "The one who showed mercy on him." Jesus answered, "Go and do likewise."

Jesus gave a lecture at each place where he stopped. People were eager to hear him. His illustrations were clear. His message was direct. He wanted people to be concerned with what they were doing with their lives. Eschatology was a given in Jesus's messages. Life on earth would be short, temporary, and an example of people helping one other to become worthy of their ultimate future. Material possessions were unimportant. What his followers had were to be shared with their neighbors. Riches were to be divided among the community of his followers. Wealth was in and of itself unimportant. The next life would not require money, status, income, or the usual expectations of the benefits of human efforts by which people enriched themselves. In Jesus's stories, expectations of the future, among the Jews, was to be a communal effort for a communal society. Non-Jews were ancillary to the Jewish community. Jesus was the spokesman for a revitalized Jewish religious movement. It was this redirection of a religious future that ultimately imperiled him.

E. Professional Jealousy

Jesus represented a new interpretation of the Jewish religion. Since he did not observe the Sabbath as required by the Sadducees and Pharisees by refraining from undertaking any activity on this day, he was classified as a Jewish "law breaker" of the Sabbath. The general public accepted him and his message. The rabbis, scribes, Pharisees, and Sadducees resented his casual approach to the rigors of the "law" that forbade any activity no matter how important it may have been to the persons involved. Jesus tried to illustrate how this observance was not followed even by these religious authorities when a crisis involved them. The retrieval of a religious leader's ox or donkey that had fallen into a well would certainly be rescued even on the Sabbath. He kept working with persons who came to him even when it should not have been done because he felt the person's need took precedence over the religious observances.

As an example of the continuing confrontation between Jesus and the Jewish leaders of his day, Luke tells the story of a Pharisee who asked Jesus to dine with him. Jesus went with him and sat down at his table. The Pharisee was astonished to see that he did not first wash before dinner. Jesus said to him, "You Pharisees cleanse the outside of the cup and the dish, but inside you are full of extortion and wickedness. You fools! Did not he who made the outside make the inside also? But give for alms those things which are within; and behold, everything is clean for you. But woe to you Pharisees! For you love the best seat in the synagogues and salutation in the marketplaces. Woe to you! You are like graves which are not seen, and men walk over them without knowing it."

As he went away from there, the scribes and Pharisees began to press him hard and to provoke him to speak of many things, lying in wait for him, to catch at something he might say.

Jesus interpreted religion as a gift from God to persons to use to help them in their interpersonal relations. Whatever a person did, or had, or felt toward another person was to be helpful in aiding that person to see how his or her life can become an illustration of the love of God that could be manifested through human experience and interaction. For Jesus, his major purpose and goal was to make his Jewish compatriots aware of their future. He too believed the world would end shortly. God, for him, was real and apparent. As with many early religious leaders, this world was only a stepping-stone to the next world. The end of the world was near for him as it was for all the early peoples. As I mentioned previously, eschatology was a vital and important part of every religion and especially of Christianity as the early leaders of the movement began to fan out across the Roman Empire. It was only a matter of time until they would meet their maker and be in some heavenly place for the rest of eternity. They had no way of evaluating or differentiating between reality and aspiration.

F. Arrival in Jerusalem

In his journey to Jerusalem, Jesus and his followers wanted to be part of the Passover festivities. He was hailed as a hero and king of the commoners who spread flowers before him as he entered the city riding on a donkey. It must have been a very heartwarming time for him to see how the local people all turned out to greet him. His reputation had preceded him. People spoke of his many miracles and his controversy with the leaders of the Jewish community. Upon arriving at the temple, he was incensed with the practice of the money changers and traders who were using it for their own profit. He turned over their money tables and scattered the shekels and coins in all directions. Needless to say, these men complained to the chief rabbi and Sanhedrin about this young rabbi who drove them out of the temple.

"Who does he think he is?" one of the money changers asked the temple's council. "He comes in here as if he owned the temple and tells us we are all sinners and destroyers of the sanctity of the temple! You've got to do something with this man before he destroys the foundation of our faith! The crowds follow him everywhere and listen to his every word. They even applauded after he drove us out of the temple!"

The Sanhedrin met to discuss this radical young man who took it upon himself to set the rules of behavior in the temple. "You should have seen the following he has! He rode a donkey into the city, and his followers strewed flowers before him! You know who these people are, don't you?" one of the elders asked his colleague. "They're nothing more than the poor, illiterate masses. We have to watch out that they don't desecrate our faith and destroy what our tradition has created. He promises them that they will be part of the Kingdom of God if they believe what he believes and distribute their money and wealth to the masses! Have you ever heard of anything more radical than that? He's undermining Judaism, that's what he's doing!"

The discussions continued for some time among the council members. They finally decided they had to do something with this religious radical who wanted to overthrow their traditions and observances.

"He disregards the rules of the Sabbath. He heals people on the Sabbath! He should know this is not part of our religious tradition! He does it even when some of our Pharisaic members have taken him to task for these actions! But he won't listen. He tells them parables about how anyone would save his donkey from drowning if it were caught in a flood or has fallen into a well! Who does he think he is to question the rules of behavior for a pious Jew?"

"What we should do is have him arrested and taken before Pontius Pilate to complain about his destructive behavior to our faith," the temple's rabbi suggested. "It seems to me the Romans wouldn't sanction any behavior that would put their control over the masses in any jeopardy! What this Jesus is proposing is a radical revision of what real Jews, such as ourselves, believe. We can't tolerate this upstart. He's got to be eliminated as soon as possible before he arouses the masses to challenge not only our religious practices but our social and economic system! It's too dangerous to allow him and his followers to preach his view of salvation! He wants to change our ancient traditions and customs of Judaism. We can't allow that to happen!"

Jesus knew his words and actions were going to get him into trouble with the Sanhedrin and Sadducees. He already had encountered numerous Pharisees in his travels with his disciples throughout Galilee. On his last night in which he held what has become known as the Last Supper in Jerusalem, he asked three of his disciples to go with him up the Mount of Olives. "I want to pray. The future is not looking very bright at present. The Jewish authorities are becoming jealous of what we're doing and what we're proclaiming. They don't want all Jews to enter into the Kingdom of God. They want to reserve this privilege for themselves."

"Well, if they want to start something, let them come," Peter said. "I've got my sword! I'm not going down without a fight!"

"Peter, if I'm taken prisoner, and I'm sure they're plotting against me, you're going to deny you even know me! Before the cock crows, you will deny me three times."

"Jesus, I'd never do that! How could anyone who's been with you these past three years deny knowing you? You've changed our lives and lives of thousands of people since we started on this crusade to reform Judaism!"

Jesus didn't say anything. He knew what was likely to happen. They climbed the pathway to the Garden of Gethsemane. Jesus moved off by himself. Peter,

John, and James sat down next to a tree and fell asleep. It was an agonizing time for Jesus. He prayed that he might be spared the prospect of an agonizing death. He knew what means were used to put criminals to death in the Roman-occupied territories. He had seen the hundreds of persons crucified hanging along the roads for offenses judged to be adverse to the interests and laws of Rome. After a few hours alone, he was aroused by the sound of men coming up the mountain. With them was Judas Iscariot. He was hired by the Jewish authorities to pick out Jesus so that the Roman soldiers could arrest him. As they came upon the scene, Judas kissed Jesus on the cheek in order to identify which of the four men was the leader. Peter drew his sword and cut off the ear of one of the slaves of the authorities before Jesus told him to put his sword away.

The guards took Jesus with them to place him before Caiaphas, the high priest, where the scribes and the elders had gathered. After questioning him and receiving answers they thought were blasphemous, the elders decided he should be killed. The next morning, they had him bound, beaten, and taken to Pilate for execution. When he appeared before him, Pilate asked, "Are you the King of the Jews?"

Jesus responded, "You have said so."

When he was accused by the chief priests and elders, he made no reply. Pilate then said, "Do you not hear how many things they testify against you?"

Jesus remained silent. It was the feast of the governor, and he would release any prisoner whom the crowd wished. There was another man called Barabbas, a notorious prisoner, who was also placed before Pilate. Pilate then asked the assembled group of Jewish scribes and elders, "Whom do you want me to release for you, Barabbas or Jesus who is called the Christ?"

The chief priests and the elders persuaded the people to ask for Barabbas and destroy Jesus.

The governor again asked, "Which of these two do you want me to release to you?"

"Barabbas!" they shouted.

"Then what shall I do with Jesus, who is called the Christ?" "Let him be crucified!"

"Why? What has he done?" Pilate asked. The crowd shouted, "Let him be crucified!"

Pilate sensed the crowd was getting ready to riot. He took water and washed his hands before the crowd. "I am innocent of this man's blood," Pilate said. "See to it for yourselves!"

The assembly answered, "His blood be on us and on our children!"

Pilate then released Barabbas, had Jesus scourged, and released him to be crucified. A just man who tried to help people as best he could was nailed to a cross and executed because of the jealousy of the leaders of the Jewish community of which he was a part. After an agonizing nine hours nailed to his cross, Jesus died. His body was taken down and a rich man, Joseph from Arimathea, asked Pilate for the privilege of taking Jesus's body after the Roman soldiers had taken it down from the cross. Joseph had Jesus buried in his own new tomb.

G. The End of the Jesus of History and the Beginning of the Christ of Faith

When Mary Magdalene and the "other Mary" went to the tomb on the following Monday, the tomb was empty. The body of Jesus had vanished. The beginning of the myth began. He had risen and was allegedly seen by a few other people. The two Marys spread the news, "An angel told us Jesus had risen. He was no longer in the tomb!" And so the legend began. "He must have risen and gone to heaven just as he predicted he would."

And so the myth started and still continues to this day among his followers.

The questions began right from the beginning. What happened to Jesus's body? Why wasn't he in the tomb where he had been laid? Could such a brilliant person simply vanish? Were his ideas, actions, and concerns for the welfare of his neighbors so extravagant that they simply disappeared? If his body was no longer in the tomb, he must have been resurrected? Where could it have vanished?

The stories of his life became more incredible. He had walked on water approaching his disciples while they were in a boat. He had stilled a storm that was threatening to swamp the fishing boat of Peter and the disciples. He had raised the daughter of a centurion who had died. He had resuscitated his old friend, Lazarus, from the dead. He appeared in remote places unexpectedly. The Last Supper, before his arrest and scourging, was viewed as a sacred supper in which the bread and wine was to be taught as the body and blood of the Christ. Anyone who partook of this ritual was to be brought into closer union with him. The impact upon the faith of his followers was incredible. If a person believed in the living Christ, when that person died he or she would be reunited with the Christ in heaven where God and all the faithful would be found! The early followers of Jesus thought life on earth would be short-lived. There was no need to plan for the future. There was no need to store up wealth or try to prepare for the long term. Life was only a short interlude between birth and death. The upper age of persons who died was around the same age as Jesus: the early thirties. There was no need for long-term planning when life was so short. The early followers of Jesus were believers in eschatology. Life would be brief before it ended, whereby persons would be reunited with their loved ones upon death. Life was viewed as the necessary preparation for death. If persons believed, acted, and behaved toward one another as Jesus had done, they would be reunited with him in heaven. For those persons who had no education, were illiterate, or lacked also the ability to think for themselves, such a pre-planned and short life was an ideal toward which believers in Jesus could aspire.

When Paul of Tarsus became a devoted follower of the "living Christ," it was also his belief that followers of Jesus would be reunited with him in heaven. As one who had been a Pharisee and a very strict follower of Judaism, Paul had persecuted the followers of Jesus and wanted to root them out of the true faith of Moses. After he had his "conversion" falling off his horse on the way to Damascus, he was never again an enemy of those who chose to follow the Christ. Instead, he became an apostle of him who would "transform lives" from what they were to what they could become. In fact, Paul—the educated tent maker, ex-Pharisee, and strong believer in the ideals and life of Jesus—became the master planner of starting churches throughout the provinces of the Roman Empire in Asia Minor, Greece, and Italy. It was his intellect, organizational ability, and dedication to following the one whom he believed was the true "Son of God" that the first churches were developed across the ancient world. Paul started preaching in the synagogues where he was originally welcomed. But once he talked about Jesus, as the Messiah of the Jewish faith, the doors of the synagogues were gradually closed to him. He then helped organize meetings in homes among people who accepted Jesus as the Christ, the expected Messiah, of the Jewish faith. Similarly, to the requirements of the Jewish faith, followers gradually had to follow a prescribed set of beliefs in order to be admitted to these newly established churches. In the successive generations, a catechism became a standard by which these early followers, who were now called Christians, could be differentiated as followers of the Christ from nonbelievers. In this earliest period, Paul and Peter engaged in a controversy over who could be a member of this new movement. Peter thought it should continue to be the Jews. Paul, the other hand, favored opening membership to anyone, including Gentiles. Unless the followers of Christ faithfully believed in the teachings, practices, and tenets as Jesus taught them, they could not expect to go to heaven and be reunited with their loved ones and share in the glory of Christ in heaven.

We need to remember the first scriptures depicting the life of Jesus were written more than forty years after his crucifixion. The Gospel of Mark was the first one that sketched out the highlights of the life of Jesus as Mark heard it told by those who might have known him or knew people who knew Jesus. The Gospel of Matthew was written twenty or more years later using some of the same ideas as written in Mark with the addition of stories in which the author made him even more special to the "followers of the word." The book of Luke was written after that of Matthew, possibly ten to fifteen years later. The book of John was written in the early days of the next century when the stories of Jesus were enshrined in the myths that people believed about what they had heard of Jesus. He took on the symbolism of a God, who, when he supposedly spoke, was guaranteeing believers they would be in heaven with him if they believed in him and behaved as he had behaved. The scriptures were written by men who wanted to convert the nonbelievers, keep the followers on the path of supporting the churches as they were established, and convert those who were not "saved," i.e., did not confess Jesus as their "Lord and Savior." It was only as the churches grew and expanded among the thousands of illiterates of the Roman Empire that the Christian movement grew and spread. The declaration of belief and support were united for those who became followers of the "Christ" (the promised Messiah and Savior of mankind). In Paul's letters to the churches that he founded, he spoke of charismatic men who had become bishops and deacons, i.e., the organizers of the churches that he founded. Initially, the Romans regarded these "Christians" as an offshoot of Judaism. Once the Jewish hierarchy repudiated these "anarchists and atheists" and their refusal to join in emperor worship, they were hunted down and criminalized by Roman authorities. It was not until the conversion of Constantine in 323 that this new religion became accepted as the official religion of the Roman Empire.

The churches grew throughout the Roman world in spite of persecution. By AD 323 with the success of Emperor Constantine defeating his opponents in the eastern Roman Empire, Christianity became the official religion by declaration of the Emperor. In AD 325, the Nicene Creed was adopted by the church hierarchy as the belief system required of all those who claimed to be followers of Jesus Christ. With the Roman Emperor having become a convert, he declared Christianity as the religion of the empire and sponsored the convening of this council. Needless to say, as the church grew and became accepted as the one true church, the need for a hierarchy became apparent even in the days of

Paul. Ministers of the word were those who converted people to the faith and were the first line of contact for the growth and development of the church. It then became necessary to coordinate the work of several churches as the next step in the development of a hierarchy. The office of bishop had already made its appearance in Paul's letters to oversee the several churches being established for purposes of maintaining the discipline and faithful observance of the beliefs and traditions of the church. Overseeing the use of funds, solicited each week from among the faithful, had also already begun in the era of Paul and Peter. It was only a matter of time until a single head of the church was elected by the bishops from across the empire to become the final authority over liturgy, belief, scripture, and the accumulating of funds that were flowing into it as the church universal. Ultimately, the chief bishop of Rome was elected pope. In the city of the mighty Roman Empire, he became the head of this growing institution. All members of the clergy, hierarchy, and rank-and-file membership were subservient to him. The growth and development of this early church began more than one thousand years of unfettered growth and control of the followers of Christ who had no opposition to what this person believed and desired. As time went on, those persons who did not accept nor wish to follow the dictates of this supreme head of the Catholic Church or who refused to accept the "teachings of the church" as designated by papal authority were dismissed from their pastoral positions. If Christians refused to accept the official beliefs and teachings of the church, they were often executed or exiled, depending upon who the person was and where he was located. It was difficult to maintain control over all these growing dissidents if they had a large following or were widely respected.

By the Middle Ages, various kings and dukes protected these dissident clergy from the official church and its hierarchy. Were they not protected by their royal followers, they would have been burned at the stake, executed, or forced to take flight to distant lands, if that were possible. The early discord among the believers within these early churches can be seen not only in the letters that Paul wrote to those who were contesting with one another over scripture, organization, and membership in the earliest days of the church but also in the ensuing centuries among the writings of Tertullian, Cyprian, Jerome, and Augustine, to name a few.

The belief systems for the oncoming generations of Christian followers were set by the pope. What had once been a strictly voluntary association of believers and followers of Jesus had now become a rigid, intolerant, and divisive association of persons who called themselves "Christians" and "followers of the Christ." The institution of the church had now become the vehicle of belief excluding anyone who did not adhere to the "official beliefs," dogmas, scriptures, and practices of the Catholic Church.

H. Conclusions

The Jesus of history was overtaken by the Christ of faith following his crucifixion. This is not to say that Jesus did not give evidence of a belief system that transcended his own life. The problem, however, was this: Did he really think of himself as the "Son of God"? Did he really promise people that if they believed in him and in his message, they would join him in paradise? Did he really expect to be transformed and transported into "the heavens" to be with God and all the faithful believers who went on before him?

The first problem of mixing the Jesus of history with the Christ of faith is the need to differentiate between reality and belief. Reality is fixed, sensory, testable, and verifiable by repetitious testing by anyone to differentiate between reality and fiction. The founding of science and the scrutiny of testing hypotheses to ascertain whether or not a given act is real or a figment of one's imagination has been established. Since it is impossible to subject thoughts, beliefs, desires, hopes, and expectations of the future to verifiable testing, one would have to reject the claims made in the Bible of stories written as facts to be credible and acceptable for current religious coinage. The facts simply do not bear out the hopes, expectations, and desires of what comes after the reality of a living human being.

Second, the stories of Jesus were no doubt embellished so that people would follow him and believe what he told them. Had his followers simply observed what he did, followed his example of interacting with all kinds of people, and tried to imitate his behavior, then his contribution to the religious dimensions of how to behave would have been a stellar and significant contribution to improving human behavior.

Third, Jesus lived in an era in which war, hatred, deceit, robbery, and death by the slowest means of ending a person's life were the common norms of human behavior. If anyone dared to criticize the emperor, governor, local leader, or any religious figure, that person would be subjected to eventual removal by whatever means was felt available, irrespective of the validity of his message. Anyone who criticized authority, especially by someone from the masses, would be seen as a threat to the authorities. Such a person had to be silenced as soon as possible so that his ideas would not permeate and resonate among the slaves, the illiterate, the masses of humanity ruled over by those who felt themselves protected by their status to preserve the social order as it was then constituted. His message proved to be a threat to the Jewish authorities who convinced the Roman overlords that this message would become dangerous to their continuing control and governance.

Fourth, the life of Jesus, as he interacted with all kinds of people, could be a model or example of how people should themselves live. Had the authors of the various books of the New Testament simply used his life as the model or guide to follow, then their contribution to a living religious faith could have been assured. But once Jesus was no longer on the scene to make his own comments or set his own example of how people should live, then the Christ of faith took over and became the dominant theme of this new Christian religion. Myths, hyperbole, excessive expectations, and fiction became the major purposes for controlling followers of a religion meant to liberate the Jewish masses. Instead, Christianity has become, as so many of the world's religions, an instrument for the enslavement of human beings to the teaching of fiction, intolerance, hatred (in radical belief systems), and exclusivity where the followers of one religion believed themselves to be superior to other religions that also proclaimed, or proclaim, mythological stories of their deity (deities) as actual facts. Reality is based on provable facts. Fiction is based upon the desired ends that are hoped for, but not seen; wished for, but improbable of fulfillment; and impossible to attain because desired ends are a part of religious mythology that has been with human beings since the beginning of time. There is no substitute for reality that human beings create for themselves. If mythology fails in meeting their expectations, they then have no one to blame but themselves.

Tragically, what Jesus didn't know was that life is reality. Future expectations or outcomes are nothing more than suppositions or desires of what might happen. Life goes on even after those who have lived their lives and sacrificed for the hope of improvements in the future do so without knowing the ultimate outcome. What his life has demonstrated is that the message he gave and practiced has now been taken over by the perpetuation of a Christian mythology making him a deity instead of the brilliant person that he was who gave an illustration of how to interact with our fellow human beings.

The church (all denominations) has made the Jesus of history into the Christ of faith. History is based on investigatory facts.

Christology is the exercise of a hoped-for belief system that people had of what Jesus should represent, rather than who he actually was. The irony is that what we know of his historical life also seems to reflect a mythological belief that he too, very likely, had that was logical given the limited knowledge and experience that all persons in the early centuries of human civilization had. We can't blame him for what he didn't know. What is depressing currently is that in today's world, all the religions claim to be the one true church, religion, or belief system without recognizing the heavy mythological content contained in virtually all religions. If persons are unable to differentiate between fact and fiction, we have an example of where we are currently within the Christianity, Judaism, Islam, or any radical sect that claims it alone knows what is real or unreal in determining human behavior.

II.
Experience

A. An Unfortunate Beginning

Guillaume and Marie Malin owned a guesthouse in Haefnerhaslach. It was known for its comfort and good food and as an ideal retreat for persons looking to relax and spend some time in the pleasant rural countryside of Southern Germany.

Jacob Rutschman had spent a number of summers, following his yearly teaching of Hebraic studies at Heidelberg University, traveling to different parts of Wuerttemberg seeking a new place to spend two weeks of his summer's vacation by himself. He and his wife had agreed they would go their separate ways for part of each summer. Her parents lived in the Black Forest region of Baden. They invited her and the two Rutschman children to come and spend part of their vacation in their home. Jacob had talked with some of his colleagues about where he might go this year to seek out a new and untried place.

"Jacob, you'd like the Malin guesthouse in Haefnerhaslach. It's quiet. There's no noise. You're up against a hill behind the house. There are few guests, so they don't disturb you. The food is excellent, and their daughter is a very attractive young woman who is their main servant. She tries to satisfy whatever the guest may need."

"How far is it from Heidelberg?"

"It's not much more than two days by coach," his colleague said. "You can take the coach the first day as far as Kleinglattbach, spend an overnight, and take a carriage to Haefnerhaslach the next day. You shouldn't have any problems finding accommodations. There are little guesthouses all along the way."

"Thanks, Karl," he said to his colleague. "I think I might try Haefnerhaslach this summer."

After the semester ended, Jacob Rutschman saw his wife and children off to the Black Forest and then made his plans to visit this new resort that was so glowingly portrayed to him. He booked a coach to Kleinglattbach where he spent an overnight in a nearby hotel. The next morning, he had breakfast and hired a carriage to take him the rest of the way to Haefnerhaslach. It was a beautiful day riding in the back of the carriage. He was by himself. The driver wanted to wait for another hour in case someone showed up at the hotel to travel the same route. The driver felt he would earn more if he had at least two passengers rather than only one. Prof. Rutschman grew impatient.

"What are we waiting for? Why don't you take me to Haefnerhaslach?"

"Entschuldigen Sie mir, Herr Professor, aber ich habt gedacht ich konnte mehr verdienen wenn ich zwei Kunden haette als nur Sie." (Pardon me, Professor, I thought I could earn more if I had two customers rather than just you.)

Rutschman offered the driver an extra amount. He took the offer. They arrived in Haefnerhaslach toward late afternoon. The driver carried Rutschman's suitcase to the front of the guesthouse where he was met by Roswina Malin. The driver motioned toward the carriage.

"This man is a professor from Heidelberg, and he wants to spend some time in your guesthouse where it's quiet. Hopefully, you still have a room available."

"Oh yes. I'll ask my father which room he should have in the rear of the inn."

Roswina hurried into the office and asked her father, "Papa, we have a professor from Heidelberg who wants to stay with us for two weeks. He also wants a very quiet back room so he can read and write."

"Take him to room number nine. It's the last one on the second floor near the stairs to the backyard. This should be the quietest room in the house."

"Yes, Papa. I'll take him there."

As Rutschman entered the front door, Roswina came to meet him.

"Herr Professor Doktor, wir haben das beste Zimmer fuer Sie. Es ist ganz am ende der Haus am zweiten Stock wo Sie nicht belaestigt werden." (Mr. Professor Doctor, we have just the right room for you. It's way to the end of the hall on the second floor. You'll not be disturbed by anyone.)

"That's what I want. Where no one bothers me!"

He accompanied Roswina down the hall as she carried his suitcase. He didn't offer to carry it. That was something every servant was expected to do. He was impressed with how strong she was. She was also a very pleasant-looking girl. She reminded him of his wife. She was about the same size. Her wavy black hair was tied into a long pigtail hanging down her back. She had strong arms and a very graceful body. *Yes*, he thought to himself, *she's going to be a big help should I need any assistance during my stay.*

Upon reaching the room, the professor asked, "What is your name?"

"Roswina, Herr Professor. Roswina Malin. My father is the owner of this inn."

"Ah, so you're the owner's daughter. Does your father serve any schnapps or wine to his guests?"

"Oh yes. He also has beer."

"After I've washed up a bit, Fraeulein, why don't you bring me a bottle of your father's best wine. It helps me fall asleep."

"Certainly, Herr Professor."

Roswina placed the suitcase in his room and left to get the bottle of wine he had requested. When she reached the office, she told her father, "Papa, Professor Rutschman wants me to bring him a bottle of your best wine."

"Ah, so he's a drinker too? I'll get him the most expensive one I have."

Guillaume Malin went down into his wine cellar and brought back the last one of the half dozen French wines he had bought while on a trip up the Mosel river that previous year. He was a little reluctant to give it to him. It was about the best wine he had ever drunk.

"Here you are, Roswina. Take this back to him and tell him it's my last one. I won't have any more until next year. The only ones I have left are German wines."

"I'll tell him, Papa. He really looks tired. I don't think he'll want any more after this bottle."

Roswina hurried off with the bottle arriving at Rutschman's door just as he was coming back from the toilet.

"Here's the wine you ordered, Herr Professor," as she handed him the bottle. "There's a glass on your dresser."

"Roswina, could you bring me another jug of warm water so I can wash my hands? I've used the rest of it to wash my face and arms."

"Certainly, Herr Professor." As she hurried to the kitchen, she thought he certainly needs a lot of attention. She was glad the other guests seemed to know where the water was that they needed and only wanted their coffee and kuchen served each day at four o'clock. But he's special, she told herself. *We've never had a professor stay with us before. I'd better do all I can to make him feel right at home.*

After resting until six o'clock, Rutschman got up and dressed. *The wine was outstanding,* he told himself. *If the food is anywhere near as good, I should have a good time here.*

He wandered down the hallway to the stairs leading down into the dining room on the first floor. As he came in the door, Herr Malin saw him and greeted him, "Herr Professor, haben Sie gut geschlaffen?" (Mr. Professor, did you have a good sleep?)

"Yes. And the wine you sent me was excellent. It was what I needed to fall asleep."

"Come right this way, Herr Professor. I have a table reserved for you just off the main dining room. You won't be disturbed by anyone. My daughter will serve you. Here's the menu. Would you like another glass of wine with your dinner?"

"Yes. It's too bad you don't have any more of the French wine. I'll try one of your German wines."

As Malin came back to the desk, he told his daughter, "I'm going down into the cellar and get one of my best rhine wines. The professor likes to have wine with his dinner."

Roswina went to Rutschman's table. "Have you looked over the menu, Herr Professor? What will you have?"

"I'll take a plate of roast beef, spaetzle, potato salad, and a green salad on the side."

"Certainly, Herr Professor. Do you want the beef rare or well cooked?" "It's got to be well cooked. I can't eat any raw meat."

Roswina hurried off to the kitchen. She gave her mother the order. "Make sure it's well done, Mama. The professor says he can't eat any raw meat."

"I'll cook his just like I do all of the rest. I've never served any raw meat to anyone!"

There were a few other guests for dinner that evening. The Malins still had three empty rooms of the twelve that comprised the inn. It wasn't a full house, but it did help the Malins make a profit from their hard work.

Guillaume went down into his wine cellar again. He found just the right bottle of rhine wine he thought was closest to the French wine his guest had so thoroughly enjoyed. He brought it to the table and had his guest taste the wine before pouring it into a glass.

"How do you like it, Herr Professor?"

"It's not like your French wine, but it'll do with my dinner."

Malin filled the professor's glass and left the rest of the bottle on the table.

Roswina brought the dinner shortly after he had had his second glass.

"Here you are, Herr Professor. I hope you enjoy what for us is one of the best combinations of food in Wuerttemberg!"

"I'll see if it's as good as you think it is, Fraeulein."

Rutschman finished not only his dinner but the bottle of wine followed by a cup of coffee and cake.

As he left the dining room, Roswina asked, "So have you had enough to eat, Herr Professor? Wasn't the meat, potato salad, and spaetzle just about the best food you've ever had?"

"Yes, it was good. I'll probably have it again tomorrow when I come to dinner. Could you tell me which way I have to go to my room? I seem to have been turned around from the direction I came."

"Certainly, Herr Professor. As soon as I clear off the table, I'll take you to your room. It's easy to get turned around in this inn if you're not used to it."

Roswina cleared off the table, and as she took the dishes into the kitchen, she told her mother, "The Professor seems to have lost his way, Mama. He wants me to show him to his room."

"What? An educated man like he is can't find his way back to his room? Be careful, Roswina. He may have had too much to drink this evening!"

"I'll be careful, Mama. It's not every day that we have a professor as a guest with us."

Her mother didn't say any more. She just thought to herself, *My daughter's a really pretty girl. I just hope she can handle herself with this old professor!*

Roswina returned to Rutschman's table. "So, Herr Professor, if you're ready, we'll go find your room."

She took him by his arm and guided him through the dining room to the hallway. They walked slowly past the line of rooms on the first floor before climbing the stairs to the rear rooms on the second floor. She noticed he felt somewhat unsteady going up the stairs. "Here, let me put my arm around you, Herr Professor. I'll hang on the stair rail so we won't fall."

"Thank you, Fraeulein. I'll put my arm around you too so that I won't fall going up the stairs. I've always had a problem mounting stairs."

"Lean on me, Herr Professor," Roswina suggested. "I'm strong enough to help you up the stairs."

They made their way slowly but steadily up the stairs and down the hall to his room.

"Do you have the key, Herr Professor?"

After some searching in his pockets, he found the key and handed it to her. "Here you are. You better open the door. The light is so poor in here I don't think I can even find the slot for the key."

He handed the key to her, and she opened the door.

"Here you are, Herr Professor. You're safe and sound in your room again. Is there anything else you need?"

"Yes. Could you help me take off my shoes? I must have had a little too much to drink this evening. I don't want to go to bed with my shoes on."

"Certainly, Herr Professor. Why don't you sit on the bed, and I'll take your shoes off."

Rutschman sat heavily on the bed. Roswina unbuckled his shoes and pulled them off his feet. She placed them under his bed.

"Is there anything else you want me to do for you, Herr Professor?"

"While you're at it, take off my socks too and help me lie down on the bed.

I'm going to sleep with my clothes on tonight."

"That won't be necessary, Herr Professor. I can undress you and help you put on your nightshirt."

"Thank you, Roswina. That is your name, isn't it?" "Yes it is."

She gently undressed the professor who had already fallen asleep. She took off all his clothes, put on his nightgown, and drew the covers over him. She had never seen any man naked before. *He certainly is a hairy man*, she thought.

"Good night, Herr Professor," she said as she turned out his gaslight. He gave no response. He was long gone in sleep.

The next morning, as Rutschman awoke, he tried to recall what had happened the night before. He remembered having help getting undressed but didn't remember who it was. He slowly got dressed and noticed his clothes were neatly laid out on the chair next to his bed. His shoes and socks were under the chair. As he pulled on his socks, he remembered. *Ah yes*, he said to himself. *It was the innkeeper's daughter who helped me up to my room and got me ready for bed. I'm glad she was the one and not Malin's wife! She's an attractive young girl.* He gradually remembered he had had two bottles of wine yesterday in addition to his dinner and dessert. He made his way downstairs to the dining room. Most of the other guests had already eaten. As he went to his table, he saw Roswina. She was clearing off the tables in the dining room. Rutschman motioned for her to come to his table. She came carrying the dishes on a tray. "Yes, Herr Professor? Do you want breakfast?"

"Yes, but I want to thank you for helping me go to bed last evening. I wasn't able to do so myself."

"Thank you, Herr Professor. I was glad to be of help to you. Can I get you some eggs, bacon, bread and coffee this morning?"

"No bacon. The eggs, bread, and coffee will be fine."

"You're the first man we've ever had who has turned down our bacon, Herr Professor. Most of our guests think it's about the best they've ever had."

"Well, I can't. It doesn't fit with my religion."

Roswina wasn't sure she knew what he was referring to. She told her mother what the professor wanted for breakfast. "But no bacon, Mama. He said it doesn't fit with his religion. What was he referring to?"

"He's probably Jewish. They can't eat any meat from pigs."

"I probably shouldn't say this, Mama, but last evening, I had to undress him and help him in bed. He couldn't do it by himself. I noticed his penis was different from Karl's (her little brother). He had no skin over the top of it like Karl."

"That's because he's been circumcised. The loose skin that goes over the top of little boys' penises is cut off when they're babies. It's the way they identify themselves as separate from the rest of the world."

"That's amazing. Thank you for telling me, Mama."

"I wouldn't say anything about this to your father, Roswina. If he knew you had to undress the professor, he'd be angry. He was a bit upset when the professor asked you to take him back to his room. Papa didn't think he should have asked you to do that."

"I didn't mind, Mama. He's a really nice man."

"Be careful, Roswina. These men can be very cruel if you're not careful." Roswina brought the professor his breakfast. "Here you are, Herr Professor.

Bon appétite!"

"Roswina, are there any trails that lead to the top of the big hill behind the inn? I'd like to climb to the top of it. Could you show me where to go after breakfast?"

"I can't leave until after ten o'clock, Herr Professor. I'll have time then to show you the way to the top before I have to come back to help with dinner."

"All right. I'll come down to the back of the inn at ten o'clock, and we'll climb the hill together."

Rutschman had brought several books with him that he wanted to read during his vacation. It was one of the reasons he took these vacations by himself: "To immerse myself," he liked to tell his colleagues, "in the Torah and translations of the Old Testament. I can't do that at home with the little children around."

What he also didn't mention was his habit of drinking during his "private vacations." While some of this colleagues suspected him of having a "drinking problem," none of them could prove it. They all liked to drink. "Jacob just does it more secretly than the rest of us" was the word that passed from one to the other of his colleagues.

At ten o'clock, Roswina was waiting at the bottom of the stairs leading to the second floor. Rutschman saw her from upstairs. "I'll be right down, Roswina."

He walked a little faster. He was pleased she was so prompt and waiting for him. He noticed she had put her braid up on her head almost like a wreath. *She looked even prettier than she did at breakfast,* he thought to himself.

"Good morning, Herr Professor. Are you ready for a hike to the top of the hill this morning? It's a beautiful day."

The sun was shining brightly. There were a few clouds drifting overhead with a slight breeze that kept the temperature very pleasant for a hike.

"Where do we begin, Roswina?"

"Follow me, Herr Professor. It's just a little ways down the trail, and then we climb the hill."

She led the way at a swift pace. "Not so fast, Roswina. There's no need to hurry. You don't have to be back before twelve o'clock, isn't that right?"

"Yes, but I can help my mother in the kitchen get ready for dinner if I get back earlier."

"I've already spoken with your mother. She said you can have the day off. So there's no need to hurry."

Mama didn't say anything to me before I left, Herr Professor. Are you sure she understood where we were going?"

"I told her you were going to show me this hill behind the inn and Haefnerhaslach this morning. She didn't say anything about your returning for dinner."

"Well, we should have plenty of time to climb the hill and still get back in time for dinner. I'll ask Mama if I can have the rest of the day off. Here's where we turn to go up the hill."

Roswina set a firm pace forward up the trail. Rutschman soon got tired. "Let's stop here and rest," he said. "There's a tree to sit on over there."

He left the trail and sat on a fallen tree trunk. Roswina turned back and crossed the field to sit next to him.

"This is a beautiful spot. We're only part way up the hill, Herr Professor."

The birds were chirping. The beetles were singing, and the view down into the valley was restful. They could see the farmers going out to their fields to gather their hay; the women were hoeing and weeding their gardens, and the children were running about kicking balls around the streets.

"It's nothing like Heidelberg," Professor Rutschman began. "We've got wagons, horses, and carts going every which way. The city is teeming with people. There are shops along the main roads where you can buy whatever you need. It's nothing like this little town."

"Is it like Stuttgart, Herr Professor? I've heard Stuttgart is really a very busy and noisy place to live and work. I wouldn't want to live there."

"Heidelberg is a big university town. It's probably not as big and noisy as Stuttgart. Your little town is really out in the country, Roswina. Have you ever been anywhere else?"

"No, I haven't, Herr Professor. I probably wouldn't know what to do if I had to live in a big city. Haefnerhaslach is big enough for me!"

Rutschman laughed. "You probably haven't even been out of Wuerttemberg, have you? You haven't even seen any of the big cities like Karlsruhe, Frankfurt, or Stuttgart, have you? You're just a country girl!"

"Yes, I am, Herr Professor. I like living here and working for my parents.

They've been very good to me!"

Rutschman didn't say anything. He got up from the tree trunk and started back up the hill. He was struggling with the steepness of the path. "Roswina, give me your hand. I can't go up the hill without your help."

Roswina extended her hand, and Rutschman took hold of it. As the path steepened, Roswina had to pull harder to help him of the trail. After a considerable effort, she led him to another tree trunk on the side of the trail. "We'd better rest here, Herr Professor. It's not much farther, but you look as though you're worn-out!"

He sat down heavily. "Let me rest, Roswina. Sit next to me so I can lean on your shoulder. This climb is more difficult than I expected."

Roswina sat very close to him. He put his arm around her shoulder and leaned against her. She wasn't sure what she should do, but after all, he was a professor and a guest in her father's inn. After a considerable amount of time in which she thought he had fallen asleep, she said, "Herr Professor? Wake up. We're almost to the top!"

Rutschman woke up with a start. "What did you say?"

"I said we'd better be going. We're almost to the top, and if we're going to get back in time for dinner, we'd better be on our way!"

Rutschman opened his eyes, and Roswina helped him up. He hung on to her even after getting up from the log.

"It's not very far now, Herr Professor."

She took him by the hand and led him to the top of the hill. There was a bench at the very top where she said, "Now you can see the entire valley. Have a seat, Herr Professor. Isn't it a beautiful view?"

"Yes, it is, Roswina. It's almost as pretty a picture as you are. If you hadn't helped me up the trail, I would never have made it!"

Roswina was embarrassed by his comment. She blushed noticeably. She wasn't sure what she should say. After a long pause, she suggested, "We'd better go back down the hill, Herr Professor. It won't take us as long to go back down as it did coming up."

"That's for sure! But why rush down? I'd like to spend some more time with you."

"Herr Professor, I have to get back down and help my mother with the dinner.

The clock on the church tower says it's already eleven-thirty."

Roswina extended her hand, and he got up. They retraced their steps back down the hill. She wanted to let go of his hand, but he held it tightly. He wouldn't let go. By the time they reached the inn, the clock struck twelve.

"Could you take me to my room, Roswina? I'm really tired out from the climb."

"Certainly, Herr Professor."

She led him by the hand up the stairs, down the hall, and to his door. As she was about to leave, he asked, "Could you help me take off my shoes? I'm too exhausted to do it myself."

"Certainly, Herr Professor."

He sat down, and she slipped off this shoes. "Do you need anything else, Herr Professor?"

"Yes. I'm too tired to go down for dinner. Could you bring me something to eat in half an hour? Before you go, could you help me take off my jacket and shirt? I'd like to sleep a while before you bring me my dinner."

"Certainly, Herr Professor."

Roswina helped him take off his jacket and shirt. She then helped him lie down in bed.

"What time is dinner over?" he asked. "At two o'clock, Herr Professor." "Bring me my dinner at two, and we'll have dinner together, Roswina. You told me yesterday you were off work until the four-o'clock coffee hour. Also, bring me another of that good rhine wine your father gave me yesterday. We'll have some together."

Roswina was nonplused. The professor was inviting her to dinner and wine!

"Thank you very much, Herr Professor. I'd like that. I'll tell my mother you want a late dinner and a bottle of wine. She won't expect me back to work until four o'clock."

Roswina left the professor to rest. She was thrilled he had asked her to join him for dinner and wine. She had never had anyone propose that before. *Should I say something to Mama or not?* she asked herself. *No, I'd better keep it a secret. I'm not sure she'd approve of his proposal, even though he is a professor.*

Roswina quickly served the guests their dinner, cleaned up the dining room, and took the dinner and bottle of wine up to the professor's room. Before she left, she told her mother, "I'll rest after dinner and see you at four o'clock, Mama. I'm going for a walk this afternoon."

She took a large tray with the professor's dinner on it and an extra amount for herself. When her mother asked why, she said, "The professor was exhausted by his tour up the hill this morning, Mama. He needs some extra food to keep up his strength. He wants the wine because he says it helps him to fall asleep."

Her mother didn't say anything. She wondered why the professor was getting all this special attention from her daughter. *Well, she's old enough to take care of herself, I guess. I shouldn't worry about her.*

When Roswina knocked on the professor's door, she was surprised when he said enter. She had thought he might still be asleep. She opened the door and saw the professor was still in bed.

"Shall I come back later, Herr Professor?"

"No, no. We'll have dinner together and some wine with it. Did you bring a bottle with you?"

"Yes, I did, Herr Professor. Mama wondered why you wanted one so early in the day. I told her you had worn yourself out climbing the hill this morning."

"Put the tray on the table, Roswina, and pull up a chair. I'm going to lock the door so no one disturbs us."

As he rose from the bed, Roswina noticed he didn't have any clothes on, only a nightshirt.

"You must have been really tired, Herr Professor! Did you have a good sleep?"

"Yes, I did. I sleep much better with little, if anything, on. Don't you do the same during the summers?"

"Yes, I do, Herr Professor."

"Why don't you take off some of your clothes, Roswina, you'll feel much better."

She took off her petticoat and laid it on the chair next to the door.

"Come over here next to me so that we can eat dinner together and sample the wine you've brought. It'll make you feel good."

"Yes, Herr Professor. I've never had anything to drink with a professor before. Shall I butter the bread and serve you the meat on your plate, or do you want to eat right from the tray?"

"Before we have dinner together, Roswina, I'd like to open this bottle and pour you a glass of wine. It's the best way to start off a meal."

He proceeded to remove the cork from the bottle and poured her a glass. "I've never had any wine before, Herr Professor," she confided. He poured himself a glass and proposed a toast. "To an enjoyable afternoon, Roswina, and one you'll never forget. Drink up."

She took one sip. "This tastes very good, Herr Professor."

He poured more into her glass. She took sip after sip before he had even tasted his.

"Isn't that good, Roswina? Before you know it, you'll want to have some more."

He kept pouring more wine into her glass. She was beginning to drink it as if it were water. She really had no idea what would happen if she drank too much wine.

Rutschman had helped himself to some of the food on the tray. He offered some to Roswina but noticed her eyes gradually closing. "Here, have some roast beef and bread, Roswina. It'll help you adjust to the wine better."

He filled her glass the third time. By now she was no longer able to distinguish between the dinner and wine, it seemed. He watched her closely. Her eyes were beginning to close. He put his hand on her thigh. She made no effort to remove it. He moved it under her skirt and up her leg. She didn't resist. In fact, she seemed to like what he was doing.

"That feels . . . good, Herr . . . Professor. Do it . . . some more," slurring her words as she responded to the warmth of his hands. He had now unbuttoned her blouse and began to play with her breasts. She became even more receptive to his movements.

He gave her another glass of wine.

"This should do it, my dear. You won't even know what happened to you this afternoon."

Rutschman took off her clothes and his own nightshirt. He laid her on the bed and proceeded to insert his hardened penis. Her well-formed figure aroused him to its fullest extent. He didn't waste any time. Before he even seemed to know it, he had ejaculated not only once but twice. She had hardly even moved during his thrusts.

"You're a beautiful girl, Roswina. It's too bad my wife can't do it as well as you can!"

Rutschman got up from the bed and sat down to finish his dinner. He looked at Roswina longingly. *I wonder if she'll remember what we did this afternoon?* he thought to himself. *Probably not. I'd better get her dressed and let her sleep the rest of the afternoon.* He got up and put Roswina's clothes on her again. He had no trouble doing so since he often helped his wife get dressed after intercourse. When he had finished, he lay down on the bed next to her and slept. *It was about the best sex I've had in a long, long time,* he reminded himself as he fell asleep.

After another hour, Roswina awoke. She had a headache but otherwise felt no different than before she came into the professor's room. She looked over and saw him asleep next to her. *Oh, what have I done?* she thought to herself. *Why am I lying on the professor's bed? I'd better get up and go down to help Mama with the coffee hour.*

As she was about to leave, Rutschman awoke. "Where are you going, Roswina?

Didn't you like our dinner together?"

"Yes, I did, Herr Professor. But I didn't know it was so late. And why was I lying on your bed?"

"You must have fallen asleep from the wine, Roswina. That's nothing to worry about. It often happens to most people who drink wine for the first time. They're not used to it."

"Thank you, Herr Professor. I'll take the tray and plates down to the kitchen.

Mama will be expecting me to help pretty soon for our coffee hour."

She hurried to the kitchen and found her mother already at work making the coffee.

"Where have you been so long, Roswina? I thought you said you were going for a walk?"

"I must have spent too much time out in the sun, Mama. I've got a headache."

"Well, don't tell your father! He doesn't think young women should be walking the streets at any rate! You're not a little girl anymore, Roswina!"

Roswina said nothing. But she still couldn't get over the picture in her mind of waking up on the professor's bed. *What was I doing there?* she asked herself over and over again. *Surely I didn't sleep with him?* But she wasn't sure. She couldn't remember.

The next week of the professor's stay was quiet. When he suggested she should join him for a glass of wine, she politely declined.

"No, thank you, Herr Professor. I can't drink and do my work at the same time."

She did take him up the hill a few more times. He kept saying he couldn't make it by himself. He seemed to enjoy his stay. He spent most of his time in his room reading and drinking the wine he requested from Guillaume Malin. He never again had an opportunity to have intercourse with Roswina. The image of her getting up from his bed never left her. Rutschman returned to Heidelberg after his two-week sojourn in Haefnerhaslach. He never did return. The outcome of his tryst with Roswina, however, resulted in her producing a baby boy in early March of 1849. She called him Gottlieb (loved by God). She thought back long and hard to that day with Herr Professor Rutschman. *So that's why I was in his bed!* She finally realized who the father was of her son!

B. The Consequences of Experience—Part I

Roswina didn't know how to cope with her newborn son. She was still bewildered with the fact that it must have been the esteemed professor from Heidelberg who had put her in this position. She hadn't been with any other man! After she had become "large with child," she told her mother what had happened on that fateful day in July of 1848.

"He must have done it to me, Mama! I didn't remember anything from the time I drank the wine until I woke up two hours later! He was sitting next to the bed reading his Bible when I woke up. I asked him what had happened. I didn't remember anything. All he said was 'It was a wonderful experience. Your father carries excellent wine even if it isn't French'."

"There's nothing we can do about it now, Roswina. You got pregnant and now have a son. Papa still can't accept the fact. We've tried to keep it quiet. I even told my friends I was the mother of your son, but they didn't believe me. It's going to be hard for him to grow up in Haefnerhaslach! He'll be known as the bastard son of the Malins! No one will know where he came from. They'll only know he's your son, and you're not married!"

Roswina began to cry. "Mama, it's so unfair! It's not Gottlieb's fault! He had nothing to do with it! He's just the result of the professor getting me drunk and impregnating me!"

Roswina tried her best to take care of the little boy. Her father would have nothing to do with him. Whenever he saw him in the inn, he told her, "Get that bastard out of here! I don't want people to know you got pregnant from a Jewish professor! They'll think I set you up for it, and I had nothing to do with it! Keep him out of here!"

As Gottlieb got a little older, he asked his mother, "Why doesn't Opa like me?"

It was difficult for Roswina to try to explain her father's behavior toward her son. "He has a lot on his mind, Gottlieb. He works too hard and doesn't sleep very well. It's best if you stay out of the inn and play in your room. I'll read some stories to you tonight after I get through work."

Her father had gotten angry when his grandson came into the dining room one day just as his customers were coming in for dinner. He took Gottlieb by the arm and dragged him to his room and locked the door. When he saw Roswina, he told her what he had done.

"I've told you before, I don't want that bastard around me and especially not around my customers! Do you understand? Keep him in your room or he'll have to be taken to the orphanage! I can't have him around here! People laugh when they see him and say, Guillaume, is that your bastard grandson? I won't stand for it! Either you keep him locked each day, or he goes to the Ludwigsburg orphanage! Is that clear?"

"Yes, Papa," she said as she choked back her tears.

He's such a nice little boy, she said to herself. *It's not his fault what the professor did to me!* She remembered each morning, when he was a baby, after washing and dressing him and giving him his breakfast, she placed him in his trundle bed until he outgrew it. When he started crawling around on the floor, she had to lock the door so that he wouldn't wander into the inn. As Gottlieb got a little older, she had to make sure the door was always locked. It was on one of these occasions that he had wandered into the inn when his grandfather took him back to Roswina's room and locked him in. She tried to look in on him periodically. She asked her brother, Karl, to check on him to make sure he was still in his room. Her room was farthest from the dining room. She made sure it was locked from the outside. Since her mother felt a certain sympathy for her daughter and her new grandson, she also checked on him when Roswina had to work. As much as she wanted to take him out for a walk, she didn't. She did not want to incur the wrath of her husband. She was fearful he would carry out his threat and have his grandson hauled off to the orphanage!

By the time Gottlieb was five, Roswina talked to the pastor of their church to inquire if she could enroll her son in their kindergarten program.

"My son is now five years old, Pastor Vollmer. I would like to enroll him in your kindergarten class. Would that be possible?"

"Aren't you the daughter of Herr Malin?" "Yes, I am."

"You're not married and have this little bastard as your son?"

"Yes, but I was raped! It wasn't my fault. I don't even remember it happening, Pastor Vollmer!"

"Well, we can't accept any children who are not born of two baptized parents in good standing in the church. I'm afraid having your son in our kindergarten is out of the question! Good day, Fraeulein Malin!"

Roswina had no other choice but to teach him herself at home. The neighbors did not want their children to associate with this "Uneherliche Kind" (bastard child) for fear he would present the "wrong example" of how children should be born. She did her best to teach him to read and write. He was actually quite smart for a boy with little or no contact with outsiders. As he grew older, he wanted to go outside and play with some of the other boys his age whom he saw out on the street. Roswina felt so sorry for him. She let him go out to make his acquaintance with some of the neighbor boys. When he said hello to them, they took him by the arms and threw him into the creek on the edge of the village.

"This is where bastards belong!" they said as they laughed and pushed him into the water. He crawled out of the creek and cried all the way home.

When Roswina saw him, she picked him up and carried him into the house. "Gottlieb, you're going to have to learn that not all people are like your grandmother and me. You have a father, but he wants nothing to do with us. You'll have to learn to live by yourself. It's not going to be easy. People can be very cruel and boys even crueler. It's best if you stay with me here in the house."

This was but one of the early lessons Gottlieb learned as a boy. When he was a teenager, his mother sent him out to buy some apples at a fruit stand at the end of the village. When he arrived, the farmer asked, "Aren't you that bastard boy living in the Malin house?"

"My name's Gottlieb Malin. My grandfather owns the Malin inn."

"Well, I don't do any business with bastards! Go on! I'm not going to sell you anything!"

He turned around and cried all the way back to the house. When Roswina saw him, she immediately knew what must have happened.

"How could I have been so stupid!" she cursed herself. "He wouldn't sell you any fruit, Gottlieb?"

"No! He said he didn't sell anything to bastards! I hate people like that, Mama.

What am I supposed to do? I can't help it if I don't have a father!"

Roswina felt sorry for her son each time he returned with some story of how he was mistreated. As he grew into a teenager, Roswina and her mother talked over what she might do for her son so that he could learn a trade in order to take care of himself when he became an adult.

"Roswina, you've taught your son how to read and write. Is there some way he could begin learning a trade? You know, the older he gets, the more he'll want to have his own family someday. He's got to learn some way to earn some money when he grows up."

"Mama, I've asked a number of local tradesmen and farmers if they would take him on, but each time, they say, 'He's a bastard. We can't have him ruining our reputations as someone who trains bastards!' They won't take him on. I've tried even going to the next village, and the same story gets around. The Malin grandson is a bastard. Don't take him on!"

It was fortuitous good luck for Gottlieb that his grandfather suffered a stroke. Guillaume could no longer use his right hand to do his daily accounting and writing down the daily expenditures and receipts from the inn. He could barely still talk, but with a slight slur in his speech. His wife suggested, "Guillaume, why don't you train Gottlieb to be your accountant? He's as smart with numbers as he is with words. You wouldn't have to hire someone else from outside."

"Na, he's a bastard! I can't work with someone who's not even been to school!"

"But, Papa, he knows how to add, subtract, multiply, and divide with the best of them even though Roswina is the only teacher he's ever had! Don't you think you ought to give him a chance to see what he can do for us?"

Guillaume gamely tried to keep up with running the inn and keeping track of his accounts. But as one month after the other went by, he seemed to fall further and further behind in his accounting. After breakfast one morning, he turned to his daughter and asked, "Do think Gottlieb could keep our accounts for us? I could tell him what to do each day. It would mostly be a matter of placing the correct numbers in the account books and keeping track of our expenses."

"Oh, that would be great, Papa! Gottlieb is a whiz with numbers. He shouldn't have any trouble at all keeping your accounts up-to-date!"

"Then bring him in this morning, and I'll see what he can. I'm not as fast as I used to be with numbers."

Roswina was overjoyed. Finally, after all these years of wanting nothing to do with him, her father was finally giving his grandson a chance to show what he can do! She returned to her rooms and found Gottlieb reading the weekly paper.

"Gottlieb, come with me. Your grandfather wants to train you how to become his accountant for the business!"

"But he's never even wanted me in the inn when he was there, Mama! Why should this be any different?"

"He's had stroke, Gottlieb. He can't do as much as he used to, and he needs someone to take over the business accounts for the inn. He knows he can't do it himself anymore, and you're just the one to help him! Let me take you over to his office, and I'll help if you don't understand what he says. His speech is not too clear these days. Even I have a hard time understanding him."

Roswina took her son through the inn to the business office of her father. "Here we are, Opa. Where do you want to start?"

Gottlieb reached out his hand to shake that of his grandfather. His grandfather couldn't lift his arm to shake hands with his grandson. Gottlieb let his hand fall down to his side. He wasn't sure whether his grandfather couldn't raise his arm or whether he simply didn't want to shake hands with him. It was not the best way to start what was to become a daily routine of going into his grandfather's office and trying to do what he wanted him to learn to do. Fortunately for both the grandfather and grandson, either Roswina or her mother was nearby to help translate what the grandfather wanted Gottlieb to do. For the next three years, Guillaume Malin trained his grandson, whom he once couldn't even stand being around, to become a top-notch business agent for his inn.

Before he left to serve in the Wuerttemberg Rifles division during the war with France in 1870-71, Gottlieb had trained a new young office manager to replace him in his grandfather's business. The wounds of the past as the village bastard were gradually forgotten.

After serving in France, Gottlieb was given a medal for valor and bravery in the face of the enemy during the Battle of Sedan. He was proud to wear this each year on the anniversary date and parades taking place on January 18 when Germany celebrate its victory over the French by creating the modern German Empire of Kaiser Wilhelm I in 1871.

Upon his return from the war, Gottlieb told his mother, "I'm going off by myself, Mama. I happened to go through Vaihingen/Enz on my way to enlist in Stuttgart last year, and I thought if I survive the war, that's the place I'd like to live."

His mother was taken aback by this proposal. "Don't you want to stay and take over your grandfather's business, Gottlieb? I'm sure we'll have a lot more people coming to spend their summer vacations with us?"

"No, Mama. When I was in the army, I finally put my 'unehrliche Geburt' (nonsanctioned birth) behind me. No one cared where I was born, how I was born, or even if I had a father. I'd like to feel the same way in some city where no one knows who I am or cares from where I've come!"

Roswina started to cry. She did so whenever she talked with her son. She had given him so much during his lifetime, and now he wanted to leave permanently.

"Gottlieb, before you go, I'd like to give you some reichsmarks with which to start off in a new location. It's only three thousand, but it's at least something with which to start your life over in this new town to which you're going."

"Thank you very much, Mama. It'll come in handy in this new town. Do you think I might borrow grandfather's wheelbarrow too? I'd like to pile whatever I have on it and wheel it to Vaihingen/Enz. It shouldn't take me more than a couple of days."

"Go ahead, Gottlieb. If your grandfather asks what happened to his wheelbarrow, I'll tell him and buy him a new one!"

"Thank you for all you've done for me, Mama! I probably wouldn't have survived without you."

Gottlieb piled all his clothes, a few tools, some bedding and books, a blanket, rulers, paper and pencils from his grandfather's office, and a coffeepot from his mother. As he left, she said, "Don't forget to write, Gottlieb. Let us hear how you're doing. I'd like to come and visit you one of these days after you've found a place to live."

"I will, Mama."

And so for the next two days, he pushed the loaded wheelbarrow for more than fifteen miles into a new life, into a new world, but with the same old hang-ups that plagued him in Haefnerhaslach. He never really got over the abusive treatment he had had from almost everyone who knew him as the bastard boy in his hometown.

C. The Consequences of Experience—Part II

Gottlieb never really got over his early childhood experiences. He found himself a place to live in the center of Vaihingen/Enz. A few of the big houses had signs on them "Rooms for Rent." The one he found first was just behind the main town square at Vischer's Wagon and Carpenter's Shop. He went in and asked, "Are there any rooms left to rent?"

"Yes. How long are you going to stay?" Frau Vischer asked. "Until I find a place of my own."

"By the day, it'll be fifty pfennig (fifty cents) and includes breakfast. The other meals you'll have to take care of yourself," she told him.

"Fine. I'll pay each afternoon when I come back from work." "What do you do, if I may ask?" Frau Vischer asked.

"I'm an accountant. I take care of the expense and receipts books for my customers."

"You're just the man my husband could use in his business. He makes wagons, carriages, and does carpentry for the whole village. If there's something that doesn't work anymore, people call on him to come and fix whatever is broken."

"Who's been doing his accounting?"

"He really doesn't have anyone. He tries to do it himself, and I help him when I can, but I'm not a businesswoman! He needs someone to post his accounts every day. He falls way behind if he doesn't post them each day."

"Where is your husband?"

"He's out in the workshop right now. I'll show you to your room and I will then take you out to meet him. I see you've brought everything with you on your wheelbarrow. You can leave it behind the house next to the workshop. It'll be safe there."

"Thank you, Frau Vischer. I'd like to rest a bit before I meet your husband."

"Certainly, Her Malin. Have you come a long way?"

"I've been traveling for the last two days. Have you ever heard of Haefnerhaslach?"

"Vaguely. My husband made a carriage for someone from there several years ago. He said he wouldn't do that again. It's too far away!"

"That's where I've come from."

She took him upstairs to his room. It was on the end of the hall looking out into the courtyard next to the workshop. There were two new wagons in the yard waiting to be delivered.

"Did your husband make those wagons?"

"Yes. They're the most expensive ones he makes." "How much does he charge for one of those?" "Forty marks."

Gottlieb didn't say anything. He kept the information in mind. *He probably should charge more*, he thought to himself. After resting a while, he came back downstairs. Frau Vischer was talking with another man who inquired about whether her husband could repair the floor of a house he wanted to sell.

"Where is it located?"

"It's down on Grabstrasse just across from the Enz. It's been in my family for many years, and the last family that lived there has moved out. It's badly in need of repair."

"I'll tell my husband. He'll come down when he has a spare moment." Gottlieb couldn't help but hear the conversation. After the man left, he asked,

"Frau Vischer, where is Grabstrasse?"

"It's about five blocks from here. If you go up Stuttgarterstrasse, you'll go right past it. It's the last street down the hill toward the river going on Stuttgarterstrasse."

After lying down awhile, Gottlieb got up and wandered down through the square to try to find the building that he had heard being talked about between Frau Vischer and the owner. He had no trouble finding it. There was a large garden with a huge house inside of a wall surrounding both the house and the entire garden. He knocked on the door. There was no answer. The door was slightly ajar, and he pushed it open. *It had recently been lived in*, he thought. There was still some furniture in the house. As he walked through it, he found the stairs and climbed to the second floor. There were at least six rooms upstairs and an equal number downstairs. He saw where the floor had caved in just in front of the staircase. *Probably someone must have let some heavy furniture slip down the stairs*, he thought to himself. The kitchen was quite dirty. It hadn't been cleaned for some time. There was a pump for cold water at one end of a stone sink. A wood stove stood in the center of the room with some kindling wood in a box nearby. The stovepipe went up through the ceiling, and he thought it probably heated the room directly overhead. There was another pot-bellied stove at the other end of the hallway that he thought was used to heat both the downstairs and upstairs rooms. There was plenty of firewood just inside the hallway coming into the house. *Yes*, he thought, *this place has possibilities. It must have been used as a hospital or something of the sort*. There's more room than any family would need. He left the house and kept it at the back of his mind. *If this place ever comes up for sale, it might have possibilities*, he told himself.

Returning to the Vischer house and shop, Gottlieb asked Frau Vischer, "Could I talk with your husband now, or should I wait until this evening?"

"Just a minute, Herr Malin. I'll go and ask him if he has time to talk with you now."

She hurried into the workshop and found her husband putting a wheel on another wagon that he and his workers had just assembled. "Fritz, hast Du geswind Zeit mit unseren neuen Kunde zu sprechen?" (Fritz, would you have time to talk with our newest roomer?)

"Tell him to come out. We need another hand to hold this brace while Max pounds in the spokes."

Frau Vischer returned to Gottlieb and told him, "Go through that door and you'll find my husband and his two men working on a wagon out in the yard. He says you can help while he's talking with you."

Gottlieb went through the door into the shop and yard. He found the three men working on putting the wooden spokes into the wheel of the wagon they were making.

"Are you Herr Vischer?" he asked the man holding the hammer. "Yes. You're the new man who has just moved in?"

"Yes. Do you need any help putting this wagon together?" "Have you ever had to put a wheel on a wagon?"

"Once when I was in the army in France last year, the wheel had broken, and we had to replace it with a new one. It's not as easy as it sounds."

"So you were in the army?"

"Yes. I was with the Wuerttemberg Rifles Division." "I've heard you men did a good job on the French." "We won." He didn't feel like telling any more about it.

"Here, grab hold of the pin so Max can drive it into the spokes to hold it on the rim. There's nothing worse than having spokes come loose from the wheel you're trying to put together."

Gottlieb held the pin with the large pliers Herr Vischer had given him. As the worker pounded the rim into place, he watched the spoke split from the stress of having the iron ring pounded on the wooden wheel frame.

"It's not going to work," Gottlieb said. "Why don't you soak the wood in water first and then pound the rim in place? That's what we did with our wagons in France. We didn't have any of them split."

"You really seem to know what you're doing," Fritz Vischer told him. "My wife says you wanted to talk to me about working here?"

"Yes. I've just arrived in Vaihingen, and I'd like to get a job as an accountant. I've learned accounting from working in my grandfather's inn in Haefnerhaslach. Could you use someone like me to help you with your accounting?"

"Now you're talking! I've been looking for someone to do that for me for years, and no one has done any better than I. If you can handle numbers like you seem to know how to fix a wagon, you've got yourself a job! What sort of salary would you expect, Herr Malin? I've given other men ten percent of my income for their bookkeeping. What would you say to that?"

"How about room and board and five percent of your monthly income? If after a month you think I'm not doing enough to earn my keep, we'll renegotiate."

"Fair enough. You can start tomorrow."

As time went on, the Vischer enterprise expanded to carry on wider reconstruction of houses and factories in the town. The house that Gottlieb had looked at after coming to Vaihingen had been completely restored to its original form. The village had taken it over as a poorhouse for indigent men who could no longer provide for themselves. To his surprise and pleasure, Gottlieb discovered the Vischer sisters, Katharina and Maria, also lived in the house with their parents. It was quite by accident. Frau Vischer had sent Maria out to the local farms to buy fresh vegetables and fruit a few weeks after Gottlieb had arrived. She was just coming into the yard pulling her wagon loaded with produce when he saw her.

"So, Fraeulein, are you selling fruits and vegetables to the Vischer household?"

"No, no. I live here!"

"What? I live here too, and I've never even seen you before!"

"That's not my problem! My sister and I take in wash from the neighborhood.

We're never without work to do!"

Maria turned and went into the house. Gottlieb was impressed. He had never met a girl who straightened him out so quickly and seemed uninterested in carrying any further dialogue with him. *She reminds me of her father*, he thought. *All business and no play. Well, at least I know who she is and where she lives*, he said to himself.

A few days later, he met Katharina going to the store for her mother. Gottlieb noticed she had a very soft voice. It was almost impossible to hear her. He introduced himself, and when she explained who she was, coming out of the Vischer house, he had to listen very carefully in order to understand what she was saying. "I'm the older daughter, Katharina," she told him. "My sister, Maria, tells me she's already met you."

"Are there any more of you in the Vischer household?" he asked.

"Yes. You've probably seen a young boy playing in the street in front of our shop. He's our younger brother, Karl. He's still in school."

Try as he might, Gottlieb made little impression on the Vischer sisters. They knew him as the "tenant upstairs." They might see him at breakfast occasionally before they left to do the wash. Other than a long-distance hello, there was no contact among the three of them. Gottlieb spent his days in the office and occasionally might be asked to come into the shop to help with a project. Friedrich Vischer was very pleased with the accounting his new employee was doing. He was actually making more money than he thought by year's end. He had to hire two more carpenters to help with the repairs to homes and barns that the community was calling upon him to undertake.

As time went on, Friedrich Vischer was elected to the town council. He relied heavily on Gottlieb to provide him with guidance in drawing up the yearly town budget. After a few years, he was elected council president and asked Gottlieb to run for town council.

"Herr Malin, why don't you run for town council? We need someone who's good with figures to keep our expenses under control. As you know,

Kreizer didn't do much of a job these past few years. We've always been in debt ever since he took over the job as treasurer. We need someone like you who knows how to keep the books and can keep a balance between our income and expenditures."

Seven years after moving to Vaihingen/Enz, Gottlieb let himself be talked into running for town council. To his surprise, he was elected. Over the next four years, he took an active role in helping other businesses achieve good accounting practices by teaching them how to keep their finances in balance between income and expenditures. The town was never in debt under his leadership. Friedrich was so impressed with what he had achieved, and he told his younger daughter, "Maria, Gottlieb Malin would make a good husband for you. Should I encourage him to come and visit you on Sunday afternoons? Would you be interested in getting married? You know, you and Katharina aren't getting any younger. Your sister isn't interested. Besides, it's hard even to understand what she says most of the time. I don't think Gottlieb would be interested in her."

Maria did agree her father's accountant had made a real name for himself in town. He might actually be a better choice than the neighbor's son who had shown an interest in her ever since they went to grade school together. In contrast to Gottlieb, her friend had stayed on the farm just outside Vaihingen working with his father milking cows and raising chickens.

"I know you've always thought Fritzle was the one for you to marry, Maria. But he's not going anywhere. Now Gottlieb is an up-and-comer. He's done an excellent job not only in my business but in helping others with their businesses. The town council has never been in better shape since he's taken over the accounting department. He'd really make an ideal husband for you."

"Let me think it over, Papa. I'm twenty-one, and I appreciate what you and Mama have done for us girls. Karl is doing well with you in the business. Katharina tells me she's not interested in getting married. I don't know why. She's much prettier than I am. I guess she's embarrassed about her soft voice. She tells me the boys make fun of her because she can't speak more loudly."

Maria thought it over and told her father, "Papa, if Gottlieb wants to talk with me after church Sunday mornings, you can tell him it's okay with me."

It was only three weeks later that Gottlieb proposed to Maria, and she accepted. They were married on May 10, 1882, in a large church wedding in Vaihingen/ Enz. Even Gottlieb's mother was invited. This was to be the first opportunity she had to become acquainted with her new daughter-in-law.

The two women got along well with each other. Roswina gave the newly married couple another three thousand reichsmarks that she had saved from her work at the inn. Her father had died. She and her mother had carried on. The business was good. They had had an overflow of guests each summer. Roswina and her mother had had to hire two more girls to help with the work. Business was, indeed, going very well for them. Roswina had been able to hire a carriage to drive her to Vaihingen/Enz for the wedding and back again to Haefnerhaslach. The Vischers, their relatives, friends, and townspeople were also impressed with Gottlieb's mother. When she was asked about her husband, she said, "Oh, he died several years ago. Gottlieb is all I have."

D. The Consequences of Experience—Part III

What Friedrich Vischer didn't know was the tendency of his new son-in-law to drink too much. I wasn't long after their marriage that Maria mentioned to her father, "Gottlieb likes to drink a few glasses of wine before he goes to bed. Is that what men usually do?"

"He does like wine. I've noticed that too. But I don't think it interferes with his work. I've never seen him at a council meeting having drunk too much. I wouldn't worry about it, Maria."

It was not the first time that she was to notice his tendency to want to take a drink before becoming amorous. *That's just the way he is*, she thought to herself. It wasn't more than nine months later that their firstborn arrived. It was a girl, whom they named Eugenia, a name Gottlieb had once read about and always liked. She grew very fond of her mother and clung to her as a child. When Gottlieb wanted her to sit on his lap as a little girl, she ran to her mother. She didn't seem to like to be too close to her father. Less than two years later, their second child was born. They named her Bertha after her grandmother Vischer. She was a very pretty little girl with dark brown hair and matching eyes. She seemed to know when and when not to sit on her father's lap. If he were sitting at the dinner table, she didn't mind going to him and sitting on his lap. But as soon as he had finished, she slid off and didn't come back when he asked her.

"Bertha, I won't hurt you. You can sit on my lap, and we'll play a game." "I don't want to, Papa. Eugenia doesn't want to play with you either."

After drinking a few glasses of wine, Gottlieb reached for his two girls and was about to pull them to himself when they both let out a cry that brought their mother from the kitchen.

"What's wrong, Gottlieb? Why are the girls crying?"

"There's nothing wrong. I just wanted to hold them on my lap, and they started crying!"

Gottlieb felt rejected. "What's wrong with these two? Don't they want me to hold them and kiss them like any other father would do?"

"Gottlieb, they're just little girls. You can't expect them to want to do what you'd like. Let them grow up. They'll change!"

Gottlieb resorted to his usual retreat with his bottle of wine. By the time the bottle was empty, Maria would guide him to bed.

"Gottlieb, you need to come to bed!" And off they went with him following Maria down the hallway to their bedroom. *It was almost comical*, Maria thought. *He wants to treat his daughters like he does me. But they're too young to understand.*

Two years later, their first son was born. They named him after Maria's father, Friedrich Eugen Malin. It was the name of the German crown prince, and both of them had high hopes for his success with such a distinguished name.

Herr Vischer had had a real shock that year. His son, Karl, decided to immigrate to America. He had read about the booming business environment of this new and rapidly growing economic power across the ocean.

"Papa, I'm going to America. My wife and daughter will go with me. I've saved more than enough money to get settled once I'm there. I've learned wagon making and carpentry from you. I shouldn't have any problem finding a job. Aunt Margaret wrote and invited us to come to a place called Syracuse in New York State. I'd like to go there and see what I can find. If there's nothing available, I can always come back home."

Friedrich Vischer was thunderstruck! "What? You want to leave this excellent business which I've carried on from my father to go to a new country? What if you don't find a job? How are you going to support your wife and daughter?

How will you pay for your return passage if you can't find a job? You'll have to learn English too!"

"Aunt Margaret wrote there are so many Germans in Syracuse. We shouldn't have any trouble getting by. We can learn English eventually, Papa. It shouldn't be as bad as you think it will be."

Herr Vischer tried and tried to talk his son out of going to America. But to no avail. Karl had made up his mind. He was as dogmatic about making the right decision as was his father trying to talk him out of going. Karl arranged for train tickets and boat tickets to America through the South German railway system that had an office in Stuttgart. It was a heartbreaking departure for the Vischer family remaining in Germany. Frau Vischer couldn't stop crying.

"Karl, you don't know what you're getting into in America. There are so many different kinds of people over there! They're not all Germans! Where will you and your family live? What if you can't find a job? Your daughter will have to go to school in English! Think how hard that's going to be for her! Anne (his wife) doesn't speak English either. How will she go shopping if she can't speak the language? I think you should stay here with us! We've got more than enough work to support you and your family!"

It was a sad farewell for all of Vischers. Gottlieb was the only one who seemed to approve. "Karl, write me when you get there. I've wanted to travel for a long time. I may come and visit you once you're settled into your own home. I might even want to join you, if there's plenty of work in America."

Maria, Katharina, and their parents cried profusely.

"Will we ever see you again, Karl and Anne? What'll we do with that big house and garden you bought a few years ago?" his father asked. "It's way too big for a small family!"

"Maybe Gottlieb and Maria and their family can move into it. They've already got three children," Karl suggested. "I wouldn't be surprised if they have several more. Right, Gottlieb?"

Gottlieb thought that was a good idea. "We'll have to give that some thought, Karl. The rooms here in the inn are getting pretty small for our family."

After Karl, Anne, and their daughter, Gertrude, left, Gottlieb walked down into the lower part of Vaihingen to once again look over the house that his brother-in-law owned. It was a big house as he remembered it before it was renovated. The garden was large enough to raise enough food for a family's winter needs. There were twelve rooms altogether. The town council was looking for a large house in which to house the indigent and elderly who could no longer look after themselves. *Maybe I could use this place for both purposes*, Gottlieb thought. *The council could buy it from my father-in-law, and we could move into it. I could manage the home for the village. It seems to me an ideal place for both our family and the needs of the community.*

As president of the council and being in need of a new place to live, Gottlieb convinced his father-in-law, the council, and his wife to make the move into this new location. It would mean more work for his wife, but he thought her sister might be talked into helping to run the "poorhouse." When he made his proposal, he got a round of applause from the council. His father-in-law was able to sell the house to the town. Gottlieb now had room for his expanding family. He still did the accounting for his father-in-law in addition to this new job of overseeing the "poorhouse."

With this move into their new location, the Malins had more room, but also more responsibility. The fourth child arrived shortly after they moved into their new home. It was another girl. They named her Victoria, after the wife of the late crown prince Friedrich, who had become Kaiser shortly before his death. Maria and her sister had to clean, cook, wash, and care for the growing numbers of persons living in this new location. Maria and Katharina had to heat up tubs of hot water each week in which to do the wash for the family and the increasing numbers of guests staying in the "poorhouse." When Maria heard the baby, Victoria, crying, she told Eugenia, "Go into the bedroom and get Victoria. She needs to be fed pretty soon at any rate. Maybe she'll stop crying if you pick her up."

Eugenia went into the bedroom and picked up the baby. She carried her out to the kitchen where her mother and aunt were doing the wash. They had just heated up a tub full of hot water to wash the clothes of some of the boarders when Eugenia slipped on the wet floor and dropped her little sister into the boiling water. Maria immediately took some clothes and wrapped them around her hands and arms to lift her screaming baby daughter out of the water. The skin was already beginning to peel off the little baby. Maria and Katharina rubbed salves all over her body to try to cool her off. The baby screamed without letup. When Maria gave her her breast, she continued to scream.

"We can put her into a tub of cold water, Maria. Maybe that'll take away some of the pain," her sister suggested. "I'm sorry, but there's probably nothing we can do for her anymore."

Maria couldn't begin to think about what happened to her newborn. She cried along with the baby she was holding. It was only a matter of a few hours before the baby died from the severe burns from the hot water.

When Gottlieb came home that evening, he found his wife crying and distressed. When he asked why she was crying, she told him what had happened.

"Katharina and I were doing the wash in the kitchen when Victoria started crying. I asked Eugenia to go into the bedroom and bring her out. She did and"—Maria started crying again—"she slipped on the wet floor and dropped Victoria into the tub of boiling water! She didn't live very long, Gottlieb. What are we going to do?"

"There's not much we can do, Maria. It's tragic, but we've still got our other children to look after." He then said something Maria never forgot nor could she forgive him for his seeming indifference to what had happened to their baby daughter. "We can always have more children!"

There were to be four more children in the Malin household. Eugenia died of diphtheria shortly after dropping her baby sister into the tub of hot water. After the tragedy, she never seemed quite the same. She felt guilty for dropping her little sister into the tub. Gottlieb and Maria then had Margaret, Elizabeth, Elise, and Karl. Elizabeth also succumbed to diphtheria just a few weeks after she was born. As the years went by, Gottlieb became increasingly difficult for Maria to handle. His drinking had become an addiction, although no one knew what it was called at that time. After his work for the city, his father-in-law, and a few other accounts that he had had for many years, he retired to their home in the evenings and drank wine until Maria took him to bed.

The letters the Malins and Vischers received from Karl in America painted a bright picture of prosperity and wealth. Karl had gotten a job as soon as he arrived in Syracuse. He wrote, "There are more jobs than people to fill them. Whatever trade you can think of is needed over here. People put signs in their windows asking people to work for them."

Gottlieb was intrigued, to say the least. "Maria," he said one morning after breakfast, "I think I'll go to America and look up your brother in Syracuse. It must be quite a place from what he's written. If I like what I find, I'll send for you and the children."

"What? You'd leave Vaihingen for some place you've never even seen to look for a job when you can't even speak English? I don't think I'd like that at all!"

Gottlieb got angry with his wife every time she seemed to nix his suggestions especially when he thought they were good ideas.

"You don't know anything about America. You brother thinks he made a good choice by going there. He says there are plenty of jobs, and living is much cheaper than here in Germany! What more could a man ask for? I'm going whether you like it or not!"

Gottlieb ordered his tickets, packed his bag, got himself all dressed up in the latest German fashion, and was ready to leave. His young son, Friedrich, saw him just before he was to go out of the house. He was four years old at the time. It has only been a week previously that Gottlieb had taken him to the circus.

"Papa, you look all dressed up just like the monkey we saw last week at the circus!"

Gottlieb was incensed and kicked him across the room. "Don't you ever say anything like that to me again!"

Friedrich ran crying from the room. It was the beginning of a long and hard relationship with his father. He never wanted to get too close to him again!

The trip to America proved to be an interesting plan for Gottlieb. He left his family behind with very few funds. If it hadn't been for the generosity and help that the town and Vischer grandparents provided for their daughter and grandchildren, they would have been severely deprived of enough food, to say nothing of the lack of having their father in the house. With Gottlieb's drinking, it was probably just as well that he wasn't there. He rarely took time to spend with them. If they made too much noise, he yelled at them to keep quiet. It was most difficult for Maria. She had to ask her father for money to buy the weekly food for herself and her children a few weeks after her husband's departure.

Gottlieb didn't send many letters from America. In fact, the second letter arrived after he had returned from ten months in Syracuse, New York. He had lived with his brother-in-law, wife, and their daughter on the German north side. He felt right at home, he wrote. Karl had a good job. He had set up his own wagon shop and had many customers that kept him and his three workmen busy most of the time. Their daughter, Gertrude, was getting married to a young man whose father owned a paper box company. In concluding his letter, Gottlieb wrote, "If I were younger, I'd probably also immigrate to America, but at forty-three, I probably don't have too many more years to live at any rate."

Two years later, the Vischer's received a letter from Karl's wife to report her husband had been killed in a carriage accident on one of the main city streets on the north side. Someone had loosened the bolts holding his seat to the carriage. When the horse he was driving bolted, he had fallen off the seat under the wheels of a streetcar coming down the tracks at the same time. It was a real shock to the Vischers, Malins, and their relatives in Vaihingen. Friedrich and Bertha were never quite the same after the shock of the news. They had fully expected and hoped their son would at least come and visit them before they died.

"Now, it's never to be," Frau Vischer cried. "He shouldn't have gone there in the first place!"

Fritz Vischer still couldn't believe it. Their granddaughter had gotten married in America. His son had started a good business. His son-in-law had reported how prosperous and wealthy the city was where they had settled. And now it was all gone. He couldn't control himself. He broke down as he thought over all that had happened to his family. How unfortunate for their daughter-in-law having to live alone in a strange country. As they talked it over with Gottlieb, Maria, and Katharina, Gottlieb said, "I think I'll go over to America again. I could help Anne with her finances now that she's a widow. I imagine she'll have to sell the business. Her daughter has married into a rich family. She shouldn't have any financial difficulties anymore."

Talk as she did, Maria couldn't persuade Gottlieb to give up his idea of another visit to America. The strain on her was even more pronounced with the arrival of two more children, Margaret and Elise, before he left. Once again, he left his family in the care of his in-laws. This time, however, he ran out of money. He had moved in with his sister-in-law. Since she had sold her husband's business, she had to watch her expenses very carefully. Unfortunately, Gottlieb discovered she was spending far more than she could afford. He had had to help her in meeting her expenses. Running low on funds himself, he wrote his father-in-law:

Dear Father and Mother Vischer,

Anne has gone through all of the money which the sale of Karl's business had provided. I have also helped her and have used up my remaining reichmarks. Could you send me a thousand reichmarks so that she can pay off her debt on the house? I've lent her money, but she doesn't seem to know how to handle it. She buys things that are much too expensive and then runs out of money by the end of the month. She does receive income from Karl's business, but now I'm also without any money. We shall look forward to hearing from you and anything you can send me will be used not only for her but for my return to Germany. Otherwise, I'll not be able to return until I have enough money to buy a ticket.

I shall look forward to hearing from you in the near future. Give my regards to Maria, Katharina, and the children.

Yours sincerely,
Gottlieb Malin

Herr Vischer almost couldn't believe what his son-in-law had written. "Here he goes off to America to help our daughter-in-law, and now he writes he needs money! What has he been doing all this time? Couldn't he get himself a job and make some money?"

"Don't forget, Papa, he has a drinking problem," Katharina reminded him.

"No, he doesn't!" Maria defended him. "He doesn't drink any more than most of the men who live here! You don't see him like I see him!" she argued with her sister.

"Now let's stop arguing all of the time!" Bertha Vischer said. "He does drink quite a bit, but he also earns good money for Maria and the children!"

Fritz Vischer sent the money to the bank in Syracuse that his son-in-law had suggested would be the safest way to handle the transaction. It was the same bank that the Schmeer Paper Box Company used. Gottlieb then had his niece give him the money once it arrived.

After returning from America, Gottlieb became increasingly belligerent. His drinking habit had now proceeded to include drinking in the morning. When Maria went out one morning to do the shopping for the tenants of the "poorhouse" and her family, Gottlieb wandered into the kitchen. Katharina was there.

"Where's Maria?" he asked in a slurred voice.

"She's out shopping. She won't be back for another hour or so."

Gottlieb looked at his sister-in-law. "You know, you're a very pretty woman.

I think you ought to enjoy sex like the rest of us."

"Now don't get any ideas, Gottlieb. You know Maria doesn't like it when you talk to other women like that," she whispered as loudly as she could.

Before she knew what was happening, he had grabbed her and pulled her down into the bedroom just off the kitchen.

"Gottlieb, the children are here! What are you trying to do?"

She wrenched herself free as he shoved the children out the door. "You children stay out of here."

Fritzle turned on his father and tried to pull him away from his aunt. Gottlieb gave him a swift kick in the stomach and pushed the children out the door. He warned them, "You children stay out of here! If you come in here, you'll get what Fritzle got!" His son was bent over holding his stomach and crying from the pain.

Gottlieb got hold of Maria's arm and twisted it behind her back forcing her to lie on the bed. He proceeded to undress her and forced his way into her even though she was trying her best to resist. The children stood outside the door. They liked their aunt and couldn't understand what their father was trying to do to her. In spite of crying, Fritzle went to the door and looked through the keyhole. He was amazed at what he saw. His father was thrusting his large penis into his aunt!

"Look what Papa is doing to Aunt Katharina!" he said. Each of the girls looked through the keyhole and saw what he had seen.

After a few minutes, Gottlieb came out and, seeing the children cowering in the corner of the hallway, said, "Now get yourselves back to what you were doing before I came in! You don't have to tell Mama what happened! If you do, you'll really get a beating!"

After the children had gone back to their rooms, Aunt Katharina came in and told them, "Now don't tell your mother what happened! Your father was drunk and didn't know what he was doing! It'll only upset your mother!"

The children never forgot what they had seen. Fritzle had become so angry with his father's abuse of him and his sisters that he gradually couldn't stand being around him. As he grew older, his mother had to make arrangements with her parents to have him live with them.

"I don't know what happened between those two, but Fritzle can't stand his father! Gottlieb doesn't tolerate anything Fritzle does! Could he live with you?"

From the time Fritzle was thirteen until his father's death in 1905, he had little or no contact with him. The last of the Malin children was another little boy, Karl, who was born in 1899. He grew to be his father's favorite. They would lie down together on the floor of the dining room after dinner and take a nap. It was there that Maria found Gottlieb one evening with their youngest son asleep next to him. Gottlieb was dead. He had tried to become the father to his youngest son, which he himself had never experienced.

E. An Unsatisfied Woman

Carolla was chronically dissatisfied. Yes, she had a husband, two children, loving parents, and, seemingly, the perfect home in the suburbs. Her husband was a well-thought-of businessman who managed one of the larger department stores in the city. The family was always very well dressed and attended church every Sunday morning. But Carolla wanted more. She made an appointment to talk with her pastor about her frustrations. He listened sympathetically. He had heard these stories before. What appeared to be a highly successful family living on a grand scale of income, driving expensive cars (her husband had given her a Buick for Christmas shortly after their second anniversary), and a summer camp on a nearby lake, to their neighbors, they seemed "to have it all." *What more could anyone want?* the minister thought to himself. And yet, here she was. Frustrated, complaining about how her husband neglects her, how the children don't listen to her when she asks them to do something. How her mother-in-law is always calling to check on where she is and what she's doing.

"I can't take it anymore, Alex," she told her pastor in one of his counseling sessions with her.

"Why don't you go back to college, Carolla? You said you didn't finish your degree. You got married after your second year at the university. It might help give you another perspective on life. You really ought to have become the teacher you said once you wanted to be. It's not too late."

"I suppose. But I'd be much older than the other students in my classes. I'd feel like their mother!"

"That's all right, Carolla. You'd be like another 'teacher in the class.' Someone who's lived and had experiences which the younger students have never had. You could be a real help to them and also continue working on your degree in English."

This was the fifth counseling session Carolla had had with Alex. Each time, she had raised a new issue. The first one was what should she do about her mother-in-law.

"She calls me almost every day! She wants to know what I'm doing. She's much too nosey, Alex. If I don't call her first thing in the morning, she gets upset.

She wants to know what's on my agenda for the day! Why do I have to tell her everything I'm doing every day? It's none of her business what I do!"

The next session was about her son and daughter. "I ask them to do simple things around the house, and they refuse to do them! I can't let them dominate my life! I'd like to have some free time too!"

The third session was about what kind of holiday they should go on. Her husband wanted to go to Europe, but she was reluctant to go anywhere.

"The people don't speak English where he wants to go! I haven't learned any other language. I'd feel lost traveling in strange countries!"

The fourth session was to discuss what she should do when her husband wasn't willing to have sex.

"Alex, I need sex! I'd like to have it as often as possible, but he says he doesn't feel like it when I want it! What am I supposed to do? I need sex. It's the only thing that really relaxes me!"

The last session was about her vague feelings of frustration and dissatisfaction with her life in general.

"I don't know what is wrong with me, Alex. I can't seem to find anything that I'm really interested in doing anymore."

"Weren't you interested in becoming a teacher once, Carolla? Why don't you go back to college and finish your degree? You've only completed two years, isn't that right?"

"That's right, Alex. I wanted to be a high school English teacher, but John wanted to get married after he finished college and got his job. I probably should have said I'd like to finish college first, but I didn't. I let myself be talked into an early marriage."

"It's not too late, Carolla. You could easily finish college and very likely get a job teaching in one of our local high schools. There's a real shortage of good English teachers," he suggested.

"That's not a bad idea, Alex. I might just like that. You don't think I'm too old to become a student again, do you?" she asked with some trepidation.

"Not at all. There are a number of ladies in the church who are doing just that, Carolla. They seem to like the interaction with the students in their classes very much. One woman told me she should have done that several years ago. She's having a great time with the students and professors."

After this last session with her minister, she thought this last idea over very carefully. *Yes*, she said to herself, *I could finish my degree and get a job as a teacher. I think I might really like that.*

She enrolled at the university that next semester and took a full fifteen hours of course work. It proved harder than she thought. She still had to cook, wash, and take care of the needs of her husband and teenage son and daughter. But her husband also thought it was a good idea after she discussed the idea with him.

"That's great, Carolla. You might be surprised how much you'll find being in class with all of these younger students. When I was in college, we had some veterans in our classes. They always had a different perspective on life than we did. Who knows, you may become a counselor to some of your classmates."

Carolla found this idea of her husband to be an accurate one. In fact, in the course on early English literature, the professor asked the students to write short stories that would be today's equivalent of Chaucer's tales. One of the students, sitting next to Carolla, talked with her every day they were in class together. He was from downstate. He was the only one of his high school class who had enrolled this far away from his hometown. Carolla sensed he was lonely. She took a special interest in him. After class one day, as they were walking out of class, he suggested, "How about going down to the coffee shop for a cup of coffee, Carolla?"

"That's a good idea, Terry."

After he ordered two cups of coffee, they began discussing some of the classes they were taking.

"What course are you taking that you like the best? she asked him.

"I'm taking a course in biology this semester. It's one of the most interesting classes I've ever taken. I never knew how much the mind can control what the body wants to do. Have you ever taken a course in biology?"

Carolla laughed. "Oh yes, but there's nothing like the real thing, Terry. You're learning the facts about the subject, but there's no substitute for learning by doing."

"What do you mean, Carolla? Doesn't everyone have to learn the content of the subject before he can understand what role he plays in it?"

She didn't say anything. She knew this conversation was going to be important to her classmate. She wasn't quite sure how to phrase what she wanted to say.

After a short silence, he asked her again, "Doesn't everyone have to learn the basics before he can know what to do?"

"Ordinarily, that's the case. But sometimes, there's a shortcut in which experience becomes the teacher of facts."

"I don't follow. What do you mean?"

"Aren't we supposed to write stories which would be the modern-day equivalents of Chaucer's tales for our English class?"

"Yes, but what does that have to do with what I asked? I said I'm learning biology, and you said experience is a better teacher than learning facts."

"Do you think Chaucer's promiscuous lady was the one who learned the facts of sex, or had she learned it from experience?"

"I still think you have to know the facts first, and then you'll know what to do."

They finished their coffee. Carolla saw that Terry didn't really know to what she was referring. *He's just too young to understand*, she told herself. "Well, I've got to go back to the library, Terry. I'll see you in class tomorrow."

The opportunity to get together to discuss the topic was deferred for a longer time than she had anticipated. It was almost two weeks later before they had a chance to discuss the topic again. As it so happened, the professor had read a few of the modern-day Chaucer Tales in class that the students had written. After class, Terry came over and asked, "Hi, Carolla. How about going down to the coffee shop and having a cup of coffee together?"

"Okay. But I'm buying this time," she said. "That's okay with me."

After being served their cups of coffee in the booth where they were sitting, Terry asked, "What did you mean, Carolla, that learning the facts in biology are not as good as experience? I'm still trying to figure that out."

"Do you have a car, Terry?" "Yes, I do."

"Do you know where Woodchuck Hill Road is?"

"I've heard of it. Why?"

"I'd like to have you drive out to my place next Friday morning after class, and I'll try and show you what I mean about experience being better than facts in learning a subject like biology." She gave him the directions of how to get to her house. "I'll expect you at ten o'clock, Terry. If something comes up, I have your phone number. I'll call you, and we'll have to postpone your visit."

Terry has never been invited to a woman's house before. He recalled Chaucer's tale about the adulterous woman. *Does she want to do to me what the woman did in that story?* he asked himself. He wasn't sure he could believe what he was getting into that morning as he drove out to Woodchuck Hill Road. He drove into the driveway and turned around facing the neighbor's house. If someone would drive up, they might think it was a guest of the neighbor. Carolla had made that very specific to him.

"Make sure your car is heading toward the neighbor's house and not mine. There won't be anyone there. I'll watch for you. I'll open the door when you arrive."

Terry followed the directions very well. He arrived at ten o'clock in the morning. Carolla opened the door for him. "I see you didn't have any problem finding my place."

"No, I didn't. It's really beautiful out here. Have you lived here very long?" "Only for the past fifteen years. Come with me, Terry. Let me show you how experience can win over facts every time!"

She led him into her bedroom and proceeded to take off her nightgown. He was impressed with her smooth and voluptuous body. Her breasts hung firmly to her chest. She had combed her hair into an upsweep so that when she lay down, her hair did not cover her face. She took his hands and placed them on her breasts. She unfastened his zipper and opened the buttons of his shirt. She was pleased he had a full crop of dark hair on his chest.

"I like it when a man has a hairy chest. I can rub my breasts in it."

It didn't take Terry long to follow her instructions. "Now take your hand and rub my clitoris. It gets me excited."

She had to show him what she meant. He wasn't sure where the clitoris was even though he was studying biology. He did as he was told. He could hardly contain himself.

"Let me put it in you, Carolla! If I wait much longer, it's going to shoot!"

She rolled over on her back and drew up her legs spreading them wide enough for him to enter. His movements were very rapid.

"Can't you wait a little, Terry? You don't have to shoot yet, do you? The longer you take, the more you'll enjoy it!"

"I can't wait any longer. I'm going to shoot!" His orgasm was climactic. He held her so tightly she had to tell him to let her go.

"It's okay, Terry. You've done our deed! Let's just rest for a while. See, this is what I meant about experience being more valuable than facts. You can learn all of the facts you want, but there's nothing like experience to really learn what life is like! Learning biology will never replace learning by doing. Sex is best learned by the experience of doing it, don't you think? You can read all about it, but it's in the doing that you really understand what it is."

"Thanks, Carolla. You're a better teacher than my biology professor any time!"

Carolla and Terry did it a few more times before the semester was over. The last time they were in bed together, her husband came home unexpectedly. Carolla opened the window, threw Terry's clothes out and said, "Jump! It's not far to the ground. We can't have my husband finding us in bed together. Once you're out, I'll close the window and have sex with my husband. He'll never know you were here."

Needless to say, this aspect of Chaucer's tale about the unfaithful wife came closer to reality than either of them expected! When they were in class together that next week, she said, "Terry, that's it! I can't take any more chances like that. My husband wondered why I was so soft, moist, and ready for him when he hadn't even been there. I told him, I'd been thinking about doing it with him all morning. He seemed satisfied with what I said."

F. Wanting What Wasn't Possible

In the spring of 1973, he was appointed by the president to become the acting dean of the school of social and behavioral sciences. He had been serving as an assistant vice president for academic affairs. The previous dean had decided he preferred teaching to administration. He left the office after the spring semester. The president and vice president for academic affairs decided it was too late to create a search committee to fill the position with a full-time dean that following academic year.

He was delighted with the appointment. He had had a hankering for administration even since he was appointed an assistant vice president for academic affairs. He liked the interaction with the administrative officials, and they seemed to like him. Both the president and the vice president for academic affairs said, "We'll appoint a search committee this next fall, and you shouldn't have any problem becoming the full-time dean."

He moved into the second floor office of the world culture building. He had the same secretary who had been serving his predecessor. She knew the people, the departments, and managed the finances of the dean's office exceptionally well. He couldn't have asked for a better secretary. She also took shorthand and typed up the minutes of the meetings of the department chairmen each week as well as the correspondence with both insiders and outsiders of the university. What seemed to start off so well became increasingly burdensome for his future tenure in this office. The university administration wanted each of the departments to draw up a master plan of what they hoped to accomplish within the next five years. The goal was to expand the various departmental programs to entice students to attend the university. After five years, it was the university's goal to increase its student enrollment from six thousand students to over seven thousand eight hundred students. At the weekly meetings of the chairmen, he suggested that each of the six departments comprising the school of social and behavioral sciences should undertake a departmental study to determine how they expected to achieve this growth and development in their departments in a five-year plan. He gave them two months in which to complete their assessments after which he wanted them to present their proposals so that he could submit them to the faculty senate for consideration. The chairmen went to work with their faculty and drew up plans for each of the department. They then submitted these plans to his office so that he could compile them for the school of social and behavioral sciences in a comprehensive master plan for the school to be submitted to the all-university meeting.

The economics department wanted to increase their faculty complement by three in order to handle the increase in the number of students who were expected to enroll.

The geography department wanted to increase their staff also by three in order to set up a full-time position for a member to teach map drawing and have this person become the full-time director of a map collection center that they proposed to establish.

The history department wanted to add specialists in Asian and Latin American history to compliment the other areas of the world that they thought they pretty well covered.

Political science wanted to add specialists in urban affairs, Asian politics, public administration, and computer statistical analyses as necessary faculty to augment the expected growth in these subfields.

Psychology wanted to revamp the recently vacated behavioral science building by the physical education department in order to expand their capabilities in counseling, statistics, and adding a new lecture hall to teach large sections of introduction to psychology students.

Sociology and social welfare wanted to hire two new members: one, was as a specialist in training interns to work with public welfare agencies and the other was to expand their teaching faculty in applied statistics.

The departmental reports were very extensive and comprehensive. In order to give a summary of each department's request to the university senate, the acting dean collapsed the request into a relatively shorthand analysis to indicate how many new faculty members were requested in each department without going into detail concerning the types of specialties and reasons why these new faculty would be helpful to the various departments. When he gave his report, a few of the chairmen took him to task in the question-and-answer period.

The geography chairman, in particular, didn't like his description of the department's plan for a new mapping center and depository. "You haven't told the senate why this is so important to the future of the university as a regional center for the deposit and distribution of maps for use by schools, public organizations, and other colleges in the area!"

A few of the other chairmen took exception to what they described was his "chevalier" dismissal of their proposals to which they and their departmental colleagues had given so much of their time and study! When he tried to explain that the entire submission of each department's report would be included in his report to the vice president for academic affairs office, they seemed to take exception to what he said. He noticed they no longer were so friendly or interested in listening to his suggestions in subsequent departmental meetings.

The director of the university library called him shortly after the senate meeting and asked, "Could you come over to my office one of these days? There's something I want to talk to you about concerning your departments."

"I'll stop over first thing tomorrow morning, Harold," he said.

The next day, he went to see the director of the library. As they shook hands, the director said, "You know, your school of social and behavioral sciences spends more money on departmental journals than any of the other schools! If the faculty and students would read the journals, it might be more acceptable. I'd like to have you look up the usage of *Psychology Today*, *The Geographic Journal*, and your department's *Journal of Political Science*, for example, to see how much they have been used by the students and faculty. You'll find that maybe one or two faculty members ever read an article or two each semester. That's all! These journals are very expensive, and I don't see why the university should spend so much money on journals that are not being used! We could save the university several thousand dollars each year if we could cancel some of these subscriptions!"

"Let me check out the journals, Harold, and I'll get back to you," he said. "I see your point."

Needless to say, when he checked on the usage of the departmental journals, he was amazed how little they were used by both faculty and students. *Harold's right*, he said to himself. *There's no sense to spend all of that money each year if the materials are not being used.* He cancelled most of the subscriptions in each of the departments for that next year.

The chairman of the psychology department had been alerted by one of the library staff what had happened to their journals. After the chairman checked, he was incensed. He contacted each of the other chairmen, and together, they sent an angry letter to the vice president for academic affairs about the high-handed method of the acting dean in canceling subscriptions that needed to be available to faculty and students!

By the end of the fall semester, the acting dean had made some unfortunate enemies in a few of the departments. The vice president for academic affairs had drawn up a search committee of faculty and students who were favorable disposed toward him in continuing in this position on a full-time basis. As members of each of the departments and a few of the chairmen arranged to appear before the search committee, however, their disposition toward him had become almost bitter. They complained he was "arbitrary, dictatorial, officious, insensitive, and lacking in people skills" to continue as dean of the school of social and behavioral sciences! Three of the chairmen threatened to resign if he were appointed to the position full-time. They also indicated their views were the same among the majority of faculty members in their departments! When he invited the chairmen to come to his farm for a picnic and party, only one chairman came. By spring of the next year, the president and vice president had made up their minds: he could not be appointed to continue in this position. They offered him a year's sabbatical leave in order to attempt to assuage the agony of not succeeding in what he really wanted very much to do in academia: continue directing the growth and development of a school or college of higher education in the university system.

G. Why Young Boys Get Excited

Ella FitzPatrick was a voluptuous librarian. She had a stocky figure, slightly on the plump side, about five feet six inches tall and very well endowed physically in every respect. The high school boys liked to go in the library as often as possible to see Ms. FitzPatrick. It was expected the boys and girls would be quiet so they could read and write without any disturbance. Some of the boys used to sit as close to the front of the room as possible. Ms. FitzPatrick did a lot of typing at her typing table next to her desk. Getting up periodically, her dress would slide up her legs revealing the tops of her thighs and silk stockings. The boys were all eyes toward Ms. FitzPatrick when she moved from her desk to the typing table. There was one boy, in particular, whom the rest of the boys were jealous of most. He was Charley, a class clown who deliberately talked or created some disturbance so that Ms. FitzPatrick would speak to him.

"Charles, you are to be quiet in the library!"

Charles immediately fell silent. It wasn't until after his second admonishment that she threatened him with more severe punishment. The other boys were jealous of him. After the third warning about not talking in the library, she took him by the arm and pulled him to the front of the room next to her desk. She had him sit on the floor behind her desk.

"You are to sit there until I tell you to go back to your seat. Is that understood?"

"Yes, Ms. FitzPatrick."

Charley sat on the floor next to her desk. All the boys were jealous of him. He had the best view of anyone of the librarian's legs and thighs! After the class period was over, they'd ask him, "Charley, what did you see?"

"I saw her legs, thighs, and sometimes her panties. She's really nice to look at. I don't mind sitting behind her desk when she sits next to me!"

Most of his classmates thought he talked deliberately in the library. "Why else would she put him on the floor next to her desk?" they all said. What they couldn't understand, however, was what Ms. Catherine Hack did with him. She was the monitor in the cafeteria after school. Those boys and girls who had to ride home on the school bus each day, in inclement weather, were to wait there until the bus arrived. A teacher was assigned to monitor the cafeteria after school on a rotational basis.

One afternoon, as the boys and girls were waiting for the school bus, Charley misbehaved by taking the hat of one of the girls and running off with it.

"Charles! You come here this instant and give Shirley her hat!"

Charley continued to race around the tables making it impossible for Shirley to retrieve her hat. Ms. Hack went around the table between Shirley and herself and caught him. She pulled him with her and told him to sit next to her on the cafeteria bench.

"Now you sit here next to me, Charles, until the school bus comes! I don't want you racing around the room taking things from the girls!"

After sitting on the bench next to Ms. Hack for a while, he slid under the table where Ms. Hack was sitting. Since he was still nearby, she left him there. After getting on the school bus, a group of boys asked him, "Why did you slide off the bench, Charley?"

"I could look up her legs much better under the table than sitting right next to her. I like to look at women's legs. That's what I like about Ms. FitzPatrick in the library. I can see much better when I'm on the floor next to her than I can on a chair or a bench!"

The boys all laughed. So that's why he did it! He went on to say, "I like Ms. FitzPatrick's legs much better. She's a bigger woman than Ms. Hack! There's more to see with her! Ms. Hack is very nice, but she's much smaller than Ms. FitzPatrick. I like to look at legs! Ms. FitzPatrick has the nicest legs I've ever seen, but I want to see as many of them as I can."

H. Use What You Have

It was a cold winter day in February. The ice and snow was still on the ground. There were patches of bare earth and grass visible over the open field through which he drove the tractor. The need for a trip to the woods to get a load of limbs to saw into firewood was getting pronounced.

"I'm going to drive up the hill with the tractor and wagon and get a load of wood," Fred told Emilie. "There shouldn't be too much snow left. I think the tractor can make it."

Fred filled the tractor with kerosene and water. He still had enough gas in the tractor to start up the John Deere Model B on steel wheels. He hitched it to his wagon, and off he went up the hillside road, across the fields to the road that the previous owners had used to drive their horses and wagons down into the ravine running through the woods. It was a somewhat steep dirt road with a large icy cover. Fred thought the tractor could handle it. As he drove down the steep hillside road, the heavy steel wagon pushed against the tractor. Before he knew it, the tractor was sliding off the road, pushed by the wagon. Just before the tractor tipped over, he jumped off over the left rear wheel. One of the lugs caught him on the shoulder, and while it did slow down his trajectory, he landed in the snow. The tractor and wagon continued somersaulting down the hillside to the ravine below. Fred watched as the pipes, spark plugs, and magneto broke off his tractor and crushed his gas and kerosene tanks before landing upright in the ravine. His arm hurt, but he made his way down to look at the remains of his tractor and wagon. There wasn't much he could do. He picked up his ax from the hillside and walked back home. His arm hurt and hung down his side. When he reached the house, Emilie could see he couldn't use his arm.

"Papa, what happened? You can't raise your arm!"

"Help me take off my jacket and shirt, Emmy. I can't do it by myself!"

"Papa, what happened to your arm? Does it hurt that much?"

"Yes. I had to jump off the tractor and hit one of the lugs as the tractor was tipping over."

"Don't you think I should call the doctor and have him examine your shoulder?"

"No, that's not necessary. Just rub some liniment on it and put it in a sling to keep it from moving. It really hurts when I move it back and forth. If it doesn't move, it doesn't hurt so much."

Emilie did what she was told. After rubbing his shoulder with Bengay liniment, she helped him put on his shirt and jacket again. She made a sling in which to carry his arm.

"That's a lot better already," he told her.

It took several weeks before he could have a repairman come to fix his tractor. The winter weather had still not receded. There was still a lot of ice and snow on the hillside. Fortunately, his hired man did the milking, cleaned out the barn, and took care of his cows each day. When he had finished these chores, the hired man, Carley Leach, returned to the woods and chopped down more trees for firewood.

When spring finally arrived, Fred's arm had healed. He could use it again. In addition to the farmwork, he told his hired man, "Carley, today we're going up into the woods and make a new road from the field to the bottom of the ravine. I'm not going to use the old road anymore."

"Not a bad idea, Fred. That old road is okay for horses, but not for tractors!"

In the absence of a bulldozer, they used saws, axes, picks, and shovels for the next two months, cutting down trees, digging up the stumps, and creating a thirty-five-degree road down into the ravine. They did this in addition to their regular summer work of haying. By the time they were finished, they had carved out a twenty-foot-wide road leading from the field to the ravine below: a distance of more than one hundred yards. Fred never had a problem negotiating the hill in the woods once his new handmade road was completed. As he told his brother-in-law, "I have to use what I have. I didn't have a bulldozer, so we had to use picks and shovels. At least now, I can do what I couldn't do before. I can drive the tractor down into the woods without being afraid of tipping it over!"

III.

Farming Stories

A. A Herd of Goats

During the nineteen thirties, Fred thought buying goats would be a moneymaker for sure. He could sell the milk to hospitals. Surely, they would prefer to give their patients goat's milk instead of cow's milk. He had read in the newsletter from the Cornell University's agriculture department that hospitals were going to switch to goat milk since it was easier to digest and would give the patients the same nourishment and calcium that they required after surgery with practically no butterfat. His brother took him to an auction where the farmer was retiring from goat farming. He had more than fifty goats to sell, plus his farming equipment, grain, and hay. Fred bought more than a dozen goats of various kinds. There were Saanen, Alpine, Toggenburg, Nubian, and a variety of mixtures. He had made room for some of them in his cow barn. He had four Guernseys, two Ayrshires, one Holstein, and three mixed Holstein-Guernseys on one side of his barn. He put eight goats across from the cows on the other side of his cow barn. The other four goats he put in one of the rooms to the rear of his house adjacent to the garage. Since he only contacted the hospitals after he had purchased the goats to inquire whether or not they would be interested in buying his goats' milk, the following letter was a sample of what he received from several of them:

Dear Sir:

If you can deliver the goats' milk to our hospital each morning, we would be pleased to offer it to our patients. Needless to say, however, we do not have the means of shipping the milk ourselves.

When you are ready to ship the milk to us, please let us know so that we may make the necessary preparations in our receiving department for your daily shipment of milk. We should like to begin with no more than two dozen quarts per day until we can determine how well our patients take to this change in their diet. We will pay you twenty-five cents for each quart you deliver.

We shall look forward to your notification of when you will be prepared to ship your goats' milk to us.

Sincerely yours,
The Chief Dietitian

Since Fred had neither a truck to make these deliveries nor any interest in attempting to pasteurize his goat milk, he did not respond to the dietitian's letter.

It took too long to milk all his cows, by hand, plus the eleven goats (one buck), he decided to let his calves drink the milk directly from the goats. The calves were too big to suckle the goats on the floor where they stood. He had to build a milk stand upon which he had the goats' stand that held them in place with a goat stanchion that he devised. The stand was approximately two and one-half feet off the floor. It was slightly higher for the calves than suckling the cows. This proved to be very healthy for the calves. It was rather hard on the goats. The calves had a tendency to butt the goats' udders as they were used to doing to the cows to stimulate the flow of milk. The butting resulted in the calves lifting the goats off the platform. In contrast to the cows, the goats only had two teats that caused the calves to butt even harder. After the goats fell off the platform a few times, Fred nailed a board wall on the opposite side of the platform from which the calves suckled. When the calves butted the goats, they wouldn't fall off the platform. It was, no doubt, hard on the goats, but at least, Fred had good use for the goats' milk.

The sale of the cows' milk helped to pay his monthly bills and yearly mortgage for the farm. There was little or no surplus income for him and his family. Raising calves each year gave him the means to use his goats' milk. The problem was in taking the calves back and forth from the barn to the house to suckle the goats. There was really no other alternative. He had to do this every day twice a day.

In the spring, summer, and fall, the question was "What am I going to do with the goats? I can't just let them roam like the cows on the pasture. They won't stay inside the fences," he told Emilie.

He had already tried this method. The problem was the goats couldn't be contained within the pasture on the hill behind the barn. The first goal of the goats, when they were let out on the pasture, was to crawl through the barbwire fence and search out the fallen apples under the neighbor's trees. It wouldn't have been so bad had they stayed only under these nearby apple trees. But once they were through the fence, there was no stopping their search for additional nuggets of enticing food that the neighbor had in his hillside garden. They also liked lettuce, carrot tops, and beans that he was trying to grow.

After the neighbors on both sides complained about the goats trespassing and going through their fences, Fred and Emilie decided someone had to stay with them and act as herdsman to keep them from going next door.

"Emmy, you're going to have to keep an eye on the goats. If you can stay with them for a couple of hours in the morning, Inge (their daughter) can look after them in the afternoon when she comes home from school."

"I'll talk to her when she comes home," Emily promised.

"It shouldn't take more than another hour or so after school, and then they'll have had enough grass for the day. I'll have hay ready for them when she brings them back to the barn," Fred promised.

And so every afternoon, Inge had the job of looking after the goats. She really didn't like the job. It meant she couldn't do anything after school with her friends. She had to take the goats up the hill and make sure they didn't go over to Spencers or Murrays. She also had the all day job on Saturdays and Sundays. At least, she could take a book along and read while the goats stood on their hind legs and ate the leaves off the lower limbs of the apple and sumac trees. It wasn't much fun for her, but at least, she got out of doors and climbed the hill following the goats. If they started for one the neighbors, she'd yell, "Get back here you so and so!" And she'd run after them rarely intercepting them before they had squeezed through the neighbors' fence. As much as she hated doing this every day, she had no alternative. Somebody had to herd the goats and she was it! In the summers, she had to spend the entire day herding them.

One Saturday, she asked her little brother to help herd the goats. They let the goats out of the barn, and off they went to the neighbors' apple trees. He ran after them and chased them back to the hillside pasture. They slowly ate their way up to the top of the hill. As soon as they saw the sumac trees, they ran along the fence line in the upper fields. They squeezed through the barbwire with no difficulty. Her brother followed them and watched them as they stood on their hind legs and reached with their mouths as far up the trees as possible to eat the leaves. Inge had taken a book along to read. She sat on one of the large rocks on the edge of the field where she could observe what was going on. She periodically raised her head and yelled to her brother, "They're drifting over to Murrays! You'd better head them off!"

He ran out ahead of them, and as soon as the goats saw him coming, they turned back toward the pasture.

Late one Saturday afternoon as the clouds were gathering in the west, the wind picked up, and the sky darkened very quickly.

"You'd better start heading them back to the barn," she told him. "It's going to rain pretty soon."

He ran up to the goats farthest out in the field. They seemed to sense what was going to happen. They turned and ran through the barbwire fence and down the hill toward the barn. He ran after them by running through the same barbwire fence. His shorts caught on a barb and ripped a hole in them. By the time he had reached the barn, blood was dripping down his leg.

His sister saw him and asked, "What happened to you? There's blood all over your shorts!"

He dropped his shorts, and they saw his scrotum had a hole ripped in it. The blood was oozing out of it.

"You'd better go in the house," she told her brother. "I'll put the goats away."

He pulled up his shorts and ran into the house. "Mom, I must have cut myself going through the fence on the top of the hill."

She saw his bloody shorts. "We'd better get Papa."

She went over to their bedroom where he was resting before going into the barn to do the milking.

"Papa, you'd better come and see what's wrong with Fritzle. He's got a rip in his scrotum, and it's bleeding."

Pop came over right away. When he saw Fritzle, he lifted him up on the dining room table and pulled down his shorts. "You've got a ripped scrotum. We've got to patch it up so that the testis doesn't fall out."

Mom brought the first aid kit out to the table. Pop took the alcohol and wiped off the tear. He then pulled the scrotum together and put a bandage on it with tape to hold it together.

"There, that should take care of it. You were lucky not to have torn your testis off on the fence. Didn't you notice anything after you went through it?"

"No. I didn't notice anything until Inge told me my shorts were bloody." As Mom told Inge later, "It's a good thing Papa knew what to do."

After a week, the wound had healed, and only a Band-Aid was necessary to keep the tear covered and closed.

B. Helper

The Taylors raised pigs as a supplement to their dairying operation. The pigs were of the Poland-China variety: black with a white stripe around their chests and backs. Fully grown, they could achieve considerable size. Since the building, which once housed chickens, was vacant (the chickens were relocated to another part of the barn), the next question was "What can we do with this building?"

"I think we should raise some pigs," Pop suggested. "We've got plenty of grain to grind to make into mash. We could also give them our leftovers. There are also lots of wild apples we could feed them all year long."

And that's the way it was decided, the farm needed pigs. Since Pop didn't have a car or truck that he could still use, he asked his brother, Karl, to take him to Taylors on a Saturday to look over what pigs the Taylors had for sale. Karl drove him to the Taylor farm and Mr. Taylor showed them a few of his most recent litters.

"How long will it be before they're ready to sell, Mr. Taylor?" Pop asked. "In about another month or so. They're only a month old now."

The litter consisted of three females and one male.

"Could you let me know when they're ready to sell and I'll buy all four of them?"

"Okay. Do you have a truck to pick them up?" "No. You'd have to bring them to my farm."

"All right, I can do that. I'll drop you a card when I think they're ready to sell.

You call me and tell me when you want me to deliver them."

A month later, the card came telling Pop that the piglets were now ready to be weaned, and he should let him know when to bring them to the farm.

"Emmy, go over to the Kellys and call Mr. Taylor to bring the pigs this next Saturday."

Since we did not have a telephone of our own, Mom had the job of walking over to the Kellys (two house up the road) to use their telephone whenever it was necessary. She usually took some cookies with her for Mrs. Kelly. She felt somewhat chagrined to have to impose on her to use their telephone.

"Good morning, Mrs. Kelly. I'm sorry to bother you, but could I use your telephone to call Mr. Taylor in Chittenango to bring the pigs my husband has ordered?"

"Certainly, Mrs. Megnin. You know where the phone is."

It was just inside the door of the kitchen. Mrs. Kelly usually left the room when Mom used their telephone. She dialed the number, and Mr. Taylor answered.

"Good morning, Mr. Taylor. This is Mrs. Megnin. Could you deliver the pigs this next Saturday?"

"Yes, I can do that. Will your husband be there when I come?"

"Yes. He said he wouldn't go into the woods until you brought the pigs." "All right, Mrs. Megnin. I'll be there by nine o'clock."

Exactly at nine o'clock in the morning, Mr. Taylor delivered the four little piglets. He handed each one to Pop who put them into the pigsty. He had built a slab wood fence around the adjacent yard so that the pigs could be outside during the daytime. There was an opening leading from the pigpen into the sty so that they could go in and out as they pleased. The food for the pigs was dumped into a trough just inside the fence where it could be filled by pouring the food into it on a daily basis without having to go into the yard. The fence was about three feet high with room at the top to add another layer of slabs should it prove necessary to raise the fence higher. The pigs could stand on their hind legs and lean against the fence.

After the piglets were unloaded, Pop paid Mr. Taylor eight dollars apiece. He didn't charge anything for their delivery. Helper was the name I gave to the largest of the piglets and the only male in the group. He was also the friendliest. He enjoyed standing next to the fence and having his back rubbed. If I stopped rubbing his back, he would grunt and rub against the fence. So long as I stood next to him, he expected to be scratched. When I climbed in the pen with the pigs, Helper followed me around and rubbed himself against me as if to say, "Do it again!" The female pigs didn't particularly like to be scratched. They ran away when anyone tried to pet them.

On one corner of the slab wood fence, there was a slight hole under the lower slab. A month after the piglets arrived, they had all disappeared. Pop followed the footprints up the dirt road leading to the top of the hill, after which they were no longer visible in the grass. He wasn't sure where they might have gone. He decided to walk up to the Murray farm and find out if, by chance, they had gone that far. Pop knocked on the door, and George came out.

"Hi, Fred. What brings you up here?"

"Hello, George. My four pigs that I bought a couple of months ago have disappeared. I wondered if they had come up here to your place."

"Well, let's take a look out in the barnyard."

Sure enough, when they walked over to the cow barn, there they were lying in the sun against the south side of the barn.

"It looks like you've come to the right place, Fred. Let me open the door to the cow barn, and we'll try and chase them in. I don't think we can catch them out here."

George opened the door on the end of the barn next to the fence. He then came out with a broom handle, and together, they drove them into the cow barn. George quickly shut the door before they could decide to run out again.

"So far so good, Fred. Now all we have to do is get them back to your place." George laughed.

"I don't have a truck, George."

"That's no problem. We'll use mine. What we have to do is get them into it.

It won't be easy."

George went into his garage and drove out his pickup truck. He had built a rack on the back because he often transported calves and cows. He drove it into the barnyard and backed it up to the barn door. He let down the wooden tailgate that he had made.

"It's a good thing I've got the rack on the truck, Fred. If we can get them in, they won't be able to get out!" He laughed.

Pop nodded in agreement. George lowered the tailgate into the doorway. He pulled the barn door against it on the east side. Only the west side was open off the ramp.

"Fred, if you'll stand next to the tailgate and make sure they don't try to run out the side, I'll drive them out of the barn."

Helper took the lead, as he always did, and ran up the ramp into the truck.

The three females followed. George lifted the tailgate and locked it.

"The male knew what we wanted them to do, Fred. If he hadn't run up first, we would have had a real problem on our hands!"

Pop smiled. "Yes, he seemed to know what he was supposed to do."

"Get in, Fred, and I'll drive you and your pigs back to your farm. You're lucky they didn't go somewhere else. You might not have found them!"

"Yes. I'll have to fix my fence around the pigpen so they can't get out anymore."

When they arrived on the farm, Pop got out and nailed another slab over the corner of the pigpen. George waited until he was finished. Pop then opened the door to the pigsty, and George backed his truck up to the door, dropped the tailgate, and the four pigs ran down the ramp into the shed. Pop closed the door.

"What do I owe you, George?"

"You don't owe me anything, Fred. What are neighbors for if they can't help each other?"

"Thank you, George. If you ever need help, just let me know. I'll be glad to help you."

They shook hands, and George drove off. "He's a really good neighbor, Emmy," he said when he came back into the house. "If he ever wants us to help them, I told him to let us know."

"Inge helps Mrs. Murray clean the house each week. I'm sure Mr. Murray knows how much she does for them."

Inge received a quarter each Saturday for the work she did for Mrs. Murray.

One of the first results of the pigs running away that evening was to see that the pigs were in the sty and locked up each evening. There would be no more outdoor activity after dark! When they were driven into the sty that first evening, Helper seemed to know what was expected. He ran in first, and then one of the females ran in after him. Helper came out again and nudged one female after the other into the sty. Pop shut the door.

"He's a real helper, isn't he, Pop? He seemed to know what you wanted, and he helped drive the other two females into the shed," I commented.

"Yes. He knew what he should do, and he did it."

Whenever he came up to the fence when I went up to see them, I scratched his back. "Your name's Helper," I said to him. "You know how to help do what we want all of you to do."

Indeed, each evening, I went up to the pigpen and made sure the four pigs were inside the sty before I locked the door. Once when I got into the pen with them, they looked at me. "You know where you have to go, get going!" I said to them.

Helper started toward the door, and the three females followed. Occasionally, one of the females came out again before I locked the door. Helper then came out and nudged her back into the sty. His name was most appropriate.

C. The Elm Tree

It was a huge tree in our yard not far from the eastern end of the house. It was more than thirty feet in circumference, and its branches soared more than one hundred feet into the air. It must once have been a magnificent tree. The only blemish on it was the eastern side of the trunk. This side of the tree must have broken off at some point in the distant past. There was a huge layer of concrete that had been placed in it to cover the entire side of the tree stump. It was about twenty feet off the ground where the branches had grown into the upper reaches of the tree. The tree looked as if it had lost the eastern third of its crown. The rest of the limbs growing out of this huge stump stretched almost as far as the barn to the south and over the upper reaches of the roof of the house to the west. The limbs to the north side leaned toward the road. It was really only on the east side that there were no longer any limbs shading the driveway leading from the road to the house and barn. The limbs were more than three feet in diameter reaching in three directions. I used to stand under the tree in the mornings waiting for the school bus during the spring and fall. Some of the roots had created a hill as they grasped the ground. It was comfortable to lean against these roots almost as if it were leaning chairs.

One July day in 1948, as Pop and I were loading bales of hay in the field next to Donlons, I looked up to the house and couldn't believe what I saw. The top of the tree had fallen over the southeastern corner of the house and stretched toward the highway.

"Pop, I think we better go home and see what's happened to the elm tree. It looks as though it's leaning against the house!"

"What? Where?"

I pointed toward the house. "See, the elm tree is no longer upright! It looks as though it's leaning on the house."

"I don't have my glasses. I can't really see it. We'd better go up there and see what's wrong."

The wagon was only half loaded with bales. I turned the tractor around, and we drove up to the house. It became evident that the elm had, indeed, fallen on the house, but the large limbs extending toward the barn had also broken down. There was literally nothing left upright other than the decapitated trunk pointing skyward for thirty feet! The top of the tree had completely fallen on the house and ground!

Since I couldn't drive the tractor and wagon up the driveway, I drove up through the barnyard and out behind the barn to unload the bales. It didn't take long. Once the last bale had been stacked in the barn, Pop said, "We'd better get out the extension ladder and cut up the limbs over the roof of the house. We've got to cover the part that's caved in. We can't let the inside of the house get wet if it should rain!"

We got out the ladder and placed it against the back of the house. I climbed up and noticed there were really only about six limbs that had broken through the southeast corner of the roof.

"I think I can saw off the limbs up here, Pop," I called down. "Then we can cover the holes in the roof with canvas until we can repair it."

I climbed down the ladder, got a large one-man saw out of the workshop, and climbed back up again. We moved the ladder next to the limbs. After an hour of sawing, the smaller limbs broke off, and the large trunk crashed to the ground. Pop then climbed up to look over the damaged roof.

"You'd better go down to GLF and get some tarpaper to replace this section that's broken in. While you do that, I'll take off the broken roofing and boards. The joists seem to have held. There aren't any of them broken."

By the time I returned from getting the roofing supplies, Pop had removed the torn roofing and broken boards. We went across the road with the tractor and wagon and loaded up boards from our lumber pile. The most difficult part of the job was carrying boards up the ladder and then the rolls of tarpaper. There was also some damage done to the bedroom ceiling at the eastern end of the house that Pop and Ernest Bochert repaired some years later. By the end of the day and before we had to break for milking, the roof was once again covered. The rest of the tree remained part of the landscape for more than one year. Pop and I sawed the ends off the limbs extending toward the barn and down the driveway with our crosscut saw. We did try to saw through a couple of the large limbs near the broken trunk but gave up. Since we didn't have a chain saw, Billy Megnin and his Dad, Karl Megnin, rented a six-foot chain saw and, over the course of several Saturdays, sawed the limbs into one-foot blocks that we split with wedges and sledge hammers. Between Billy's need for firewood and ours, we had plenty of firewood over the winter. We still have pictures of the stump of the elm tree and its huge limbs as a backdrop for family picnics over the course of that next year. As I've mentioned, the limbs were finally sawed, split, and hauled away for firewood. The thirty-by-thirty foot stump remained part of the scene for the next ten years. Pop, in his retirement, finally burned it off and reseeded the mound with grass upon which it had stood. Persons who later came to the farm never knew what kind of tree it was nor how large an elm tree once stood in our yard.

D. The Dangers of Giving Birth Alone

The cows all wandered down to the barn at five o'clock in the afternoon in time for milking. One was missing. Molly wasn't among the herd, but since she was expecting, there seemed to be no hurry in finding her. We milked the cows, put the milk cans into the milk cooler, and had a bite to eat. Volkmar and I then walked back up the dirt road leading to the top of the hill. The two pastures ran across the hilltop and along the front of the woodlot on the southern end of the farm. We walked up to the fields first and looked around. We didn't see her. The line of hills blocked the view of the woodlot. Volkmar suggested, "We'd better go up to the woodlot and see if she's somewhere near the fence along the woods. We can't see her from here until we cross that line of hills."

We continued up the field and reached the tree line next to the Murrays' woods. She wasn't in that corner of the lot. We walked along the fence line bordering the woods, and by the time we had gone halfway across the field, we could see her standing and grazing as if nothing untoward was taking place. As we approached her, she raised her head and looked at us. It was then that we noticed something sticking out her rear. She seemed glad to see us. It was then that we saw the problem she was having. She had tried to give birth to her bull calf. The only problem was the calf's left leg was not sticking out of her uterus, only the right one. This leg had failed to move forward out of her uterus with the other one. Only when both feet come out simultaneously is a cow able to push the calf out by herself. As it was, however, the calf was stuck. It was no longer alive. It was hanging out by its head, front shoulders and one foot straight out. It was the maximum position of strain for the cow in giving birth. The chest cavity of the calf is the broadest part descending the uterus. Therefore, if both front legs do not precede the head and chest, the calf remains literally imprisoned in its mother's uterus. It was a terrible sight to see. The cow was obviously in pain. There was nothing she could do by herself.

"The calf must have been hanging out for some time," Volkmar said. "It's dead. It couldn't survive when it's stuck because it can't breathe from the tightness of the aperture. The front feet must be lined up in such a way that when a cow squeezes, the calf tumbles out in a rush of fluids. When both front legs are not together with the head lying on top of them, there's no way the calf can exit from the cow's uterus. She must have had that calf sticking out of her for some time," Volkmar said. "Let's drive her down to the barn and put her in a stanchion so she can't move away. The only thing we can do is try to push the calf back in again and get the other foot together with the one sticking out and pull it out of her. She won't be able to take too much more of this pain."

We drove her down to the barn, and once she was in the stanchion, she lay down, and Volk pushed the calf back into her again in order to reach the other foot. Molly was stretched out on the floor. Volk pushed the dead calf back into the uterus and got hold of the other foot. He then pulled both of them together as Molly pushed the calf out. It proved successful. Not only did the calf come out, but a pile of afterbirth fell out on top of it. It was a dead bull calf. Volkmar left the cow where she lay and dragged the dead calf outside. We buried it in the field adjacent to the barn.

Molly continued lying on the floor. She eventually got up, and the remaining afterbirth tumbled out as well. Since there was no calf to suckle, Volkmar milked her and gave some of the milk to the dogs. The rest of it was poured out on the ground. He had to do this for three days before Molly's milk could be used with that of the other cows for shipment to the milk plant. Molly was one of our best milk producers.

When Volkmar entered the army in 1942, Pop and Mom took over the milking. When Molly came in heat again, she was bred by the technician form the Artificial Breeders Association using the semen from a purebred Guernsey bull. The next calf that Molly had was also a bull calf. Not only did the calf come out relatively easily (Pop assisted), but the entire uterus sack containing the calf came out as well. Mom had to go over to Donlons (they had bought the Kelly farm) and call Dr. Anderson, the veterinarian, to come and take a look at Molly. After he examined her, he said, "The only thing we can do, Fred, is push the uterus back in again and sew a couple of strings across her labia to keep the uterus from falling out again. I don't think she'll ever have any more calves in this condition."

And so another of our best cows had to be sold for beef instead of continuing to produce forty quarts of milk a day.

E. A New Bicycle

For my fourteenth birthday, Pop gave me seventy-five dollars. I had begun working on the farm after Volkmar left for the army on August 1, 1942. Pop was working at the Continental Can Company as a tool and die maker. Actually, he had already begun working as a tool and die maker in 1939. He had learned the trade in Germany before World War I. In 1939, Pop worked out an agreement with Tom Brady to work our farm on shares. Tom has the two Hall brothers, Jimmy and Joe, working for him as well as their father, Ed. After Tom and his hired men had milked Tom's cows, they came over to our farm to do the same. It worked out quite well for a year and one-half, after which Tom wanted out of the arrangement. It was getting to be too much for him especially driving back and forth from the Green Lakes Road to the county line every day, twice a day to milk the cows, plant the fields, and do the haying. He felt it was no longer worth his time and energy and wanted out of the arrangement.

Pop didn't have much choice. There was only Mom and I to help on the farm until the fall of 1940. That was when Volkmar came back to the farm and helped with the farmwork each day before going off to the College of Forestry with Dave Caldwell. Dave was also a student at the college and drove back and forth from his home in Canastota. Pop had talked with Volkmar about coming back to live on the farm and help with the chores after Tom Brady quit the shares arrangement. Volkmar had lived at our Aunt and Uncle Haussmanns on the north side of Syracuse and walked back and forth to the university. His return to the farm was a big help to all of us. Volkmar helped with the milking and then, after breakfast, went with Dave to the College of Forestry to his classes. In the late afternoon, they came back and Volkmar helped with the evening chores.

After graduating from the College of Forestry in May 1941, Volkmar worked on the farm full-time. The war was raging in Europe and North Africa. Since he was not yet twenty-one years of age, he couldn't be commissioned a Second Lieutenant after completing his ROTC program at Syracuse University. He, therefore, worked on the farm full-time. He relieved me of the morning chores, and I only helped after returning from school in the later afternoon. By the time Pop came home from work, there was nothing more he had to do on the farm.

In fact, Pop was so glad to have Volkmar on the farm that he bought a Hindman milking machine to help with the daily milking chore. I only helped with feeding the cows and pumping water for them when they went outside for exercise and watering. Volkmar did all the chores inside the barn.

By the summer of 1942, Volkmar was of an age to be commissioned as a second lieutenant in the army, and the job of working on the farm again fell upon Mom, Pop, and me. It was, therefore, on my fourteenth birthday in 1942 that I received the seventy-five dollars from Pop as a reward for my help doing the farmwork before and after school. By the following March, Pop had written a letter to the principal, Mr. Raymond Van Giesen, requesting that I be permitted to drop out of school for the spring in order to do the work on the farm of plowing, disking, dragging, and helping to plant the crops. I would be back in school the following September, Pop wrote. Fortunately for me, Mr. Van Giesen wrote back and suggested, instead of dropping out of school completely for the spring term, I should take my books with me and study them as best I could in order to take the class exams in June. If I passed them, I could stay with my class. I was lucky enough to pass my tests and stay with my class.

Pop originally thought I would buy a purebred heifer under the 4-H Club's student program and raise it to improve our stock. However, since we didn't have a car and I had no way to attend the weekly meetings, he realized I couldn't carry out the project even if I wanted to do so. The student had to be a participating member of the 4-H Club in order to qualify for the heifer project. Subsequently, that next spring, I arranged with Mrs. Jo Parks (the neighbors who had bought the Spencer property) to take me to a bicycle shop in Syracuse to buy a new bicycle. I wanted to be able to ride to Mycenae to visit my friends Bob, Johnny, and Harold. Jo Parks very graciously consented, and I bought a new bike that we put in the trunk of her car for the trip back to the farm. Whenever I had some spare time or on a Sunday, I'd ride my bicycle up to Mycenae. It was also the time Don Farrell and his father-in-law, Fred Kile, had purchased the Brentlinger farm the year before. The Farrells had a very pretty youngest daughter, Betty, with whom I was infatuated with the first time I saw her. I used to ride my bicycle up to the Farrell farm each day after chores to "talk with Mr. Farrell" who liked to sit outside each evening after supper and read the newspaper. I ostensibly visited him, but I really hoped Betty would come out and join us. She occasionally did. By the time dusk had fallen, I'd be on my way home again. These visits continued for the first year I had my bicycle. As the heat of the summer came in July of 1944, however, I decided I'd ride it over to Green Lakes State Park and go swimming on a Sunday afternoon. I arrived around two o'clock, put my bicycle into a wooded area just off the beach, and went swimming for a couple of hours. Toward four o'clock, I went back into the bathhouse to change into my shirt and shorts for the ride home. I went to the place I had left my bicycle, and it wasn't there! I looked in the woods, thinking someone had pushed it farther off the beach. It never occurred to me to buy a lock for my bicycle. I thought there would not be a problem of someone stealing it! *Surely, no one would do such a thing*, I kept telling myself. I told the attendant in the bathhouse (Mrs. Brady), "I can't find my bicycle, Mrs. Brady. What should I do?"

"I'll report it to the police, Fritz, but if you don't have the serial number or anyway of claiming it's yours, you probably won't get it back again. I'm sorry someone took it, but that's the way some people are. They steal what belongs to someone else!"

"I guess I'll have to walk home. My sister and I used to walk over here and back again. I thought I'd never have to do that again with my new bicycle!"

Thereafter, whenever I wanted to go swimming in the summertime, I had to wait for someone to take me or walk back and forth from the farm (a little over three miles). When the temperature is over ninety and you have to walk that distance over and back, I soon decided it wasn't worth it. I filled the zinc tub at the well each morning and set it out in the sun to warm up. By the time I was ready to sit in it and take a cool bath around eight o'clock each evening, I felt it was better than walking the six plus miles over and back to Green Lakes on a hot day! Someone made off with a good bicycle.

F. The Auction

Our neighbors to the east had been farming for more than sixty years. The farm originally belonged to the wife's family, but became known as "The Murray Farm" after their two sons were born. It was assumed the boys would continue to own and operate the dairy farm after their parents were gone. Tragically, the oldest son, Paul, stepped on a nail as young adult and died from lockjaw. George and Marian were never quite the same after his death. Paul was the brightest and best prepared to manage the farm. He finished high school with high honors, and while his teachers urged him to go on to college, he declined.

"My folks aren't getting any younger, and since I like farming and we have an expanding herd of cows, my brother Kenny and I will be taking over one of these years. Dad's been a big help first to his father-in-law and now to us. No, thanks, Ms. Doerr. I think I'll stick with dairy farming."

Paul's younger brother, Kenny, was a very likable boy. He got along well with just about anyone who came to the Murray farm. He wasn't much interested in school, however. In fact, after eighth grade, he dropped out. When his mother asked him, "Kenneth, why don't you go on to high school? Paul did. He's much better than your Dad in figuring out the monthly income and expenses on the farm. You could be like him and finish high school."

"Marian (he had always called her by her first name), I'm not interested in going for any more schooling! Besides, Paul is a lot smarter than me. He knows how to handle the expenses on the farm. No. What's the use in doing something I hate and am not good at? I don't need any more schooling!"

His mother didn't pursue the discussion anymore. She knew her son would only get angrier the more she talked with him about going to high school! She and her husband had only gone through the one-room school until the eighth grade themselves. She wasn't going to get him any more upset than he already was. *No*, she told herself. *If he only wants to go to the eighth grade, then that's all he's going to do.*

After Paul's death, George hired Floyd Cloud to help on the farm. Floyd was an excellent worker who enjoyed farming almost as much as the Murray family. They set him up in a two-room bunkhouse between the dairy barn and the workshop. He did his own cooking and housekeeping and used the nearby pump for water and the outhouse next to the workshop. Floyd said, "I couldn't have it any better than I have here!" He had spent some time in prison for theft as a boy. He was glad to be out and working on the Murray farm. It was just what he preferred more than anything else.

Shortly after World War II, Kenny grew increasingly disinterested in farming for a living. He got married to a farm girl from Perryville. They then built themselves a house across the road from his parents, just off Tuscarora Road. It was on the eastern end of their fields on the north side of Route 5. For some years, Kenny did odd jobs for neighbors such as helping them with haying and cutting wood. Fortunately for him, he had a draft deferment during World War II helping his father and hired man work the farm. After the war, Kenny got a job at General Electric and only worked sporadically on the farm in the evenings and weekends.

After their hired man, Floyd, left in 1946, George had only himself to milk the cows twice a day. Kenny helped after work to do all the plowing, planting, and harvesting of the crops each year. It was during the winter of 1946-47 that George became ill. After being diagnosed with leukemia, Kenny helped as much as he could on the farm besides going to work every day.

"Dad, I don't know how long I can continue working both here on the farm and at GE. Maybe you ought to sell off the herd, and we'll just do some crop farming from now on. You've got plenty of hay to harvest each summer, and if you plant some corn and soybeans each spring, you and Marian will have enough to live on."

"You're not interested in taking over the farm, Kenneth?"

"Sure I am, Dad. But I don't want to do any dairy farming anymore. It just takes up too much of my time."

George and Marian talked it over at some length. It was another heartbreaker for Marian.

"If only Paul were still alive, George, we wouldn't have this problem. This farm has had a dairy on it for three generations, and now Kenneth wants to just give it up?" Marian started crying. Every time she mentioned Paul's name, she couldn't control her heartache. "What are we going to do, George? Your leukemia isn't going to get any better." She burst into another round of tears.

"Now, Marian, there's nothing we can do ourselves anymore. We'll have to have an auction and sell the cows, horses, and some of the machinery. We might even be able to sell some land along the highway across the road. People are often stopping and asking if they could buy a lot. I can't do the farming myself anymore."

"Okay, George." Marian swallowed hard to try to keep back her tears. "Why does everything have to happen to us all at once? We've had a very good life here on the farm. Mother would be greatly disappointed if she knew we were about to quit producing milk on this farm. Her grandfather had been one of the first to bring Holsteins into the county!"

George walked out of the kitchen. He couldn't bear to see his wife crying. *There's not much else we can do*, he told himself. *If I didn't have this leukemia, we could have kept going by ourselves for a few more years. Well, I can't change that. I'll have to contact the auctioneer tomorrow and set up a time for the auction.*

George called the auctioneer that next morning, "Leonard what's your schedule like this next week? I'd like to have you conduct an auction for my dairy and assorted machinery which I won't need any more. I'm giving up dairying. I can't do all of the work anymore. I've got what the doctor calls leukemia."

"I'm sorry to hear that, George. Sure, when would you like to have me come?"

"By next Thursday, I should have things ready to go. Is your rate still the same as it was two years ago?"

"Yes, it is, George. I'll stop by tomorrow, and you can show me what you're selling and where it would be the best place to hold the auction. You've got an ideal location right along Route 5, and you've got plenty of room to park, as I recall."

"All right, Leonard. I'll see you tomorrow morning around ten o'clock. Is that a good time for you?"

"Yes, it is George. "I'll see you tomorrow."

George had to get his machinery together that he wanted to sell. Since he was going out of dairying, he wouldn't need his silo filler any more. He harnessed his horses and went to the machine shed. The equipment was neatly stored where he had left it the year before. He backed his horses along each side of the hitching pole on each of the machines he felt he no longer needed, climbed on the seat, and drove the horses as they pulled them out into the yard. He thought if there were too many farmers for Leonard's folding chairs (he had said he would bring about fifty of them), they could sit on his machinery. After the cow auction, they wouldn't have to go anywhere else. They could just stay where they were. In looking over his equipment, George had to make a decision. What equipment would he no longer need on the farm if he sold his dairy? I won't need my milking machines any more. I guess I can keep my corn planter. I won't need my harvesting, or silo filling equipment. I won't need the old McCormick-Deering tractor any more either. It was one of the major pieces of farm machinery he had inherited from his father-in-law in the nineteen twenties. It was still running well, and he had used it to help his neighbors fill their silos. It ran the silo filler. It took a powerful tractor to chop up the corn in the chopper and then blow the ensilage into the tops of the seventy-to-eighty-foot-high silos. He often thought back to the time his neighbor had complimented him on how well his tractor and machinery was running.

"You take good care of your equipment, George. To have a tractor that old still running as if it were built yesterday is really remarkable!"

George had a knack for working on machinery. If there had ever been a part broken or needed to be fixed, George could do it. He had all the tools necessary to repair whatever had to be fixed. He also had an old Model T truck that he kept running for many years after Ford stopped making them. His mechanical expertise was so great even persons living some miles away came to him for help in fixing their old cars and trucks.

He had three hay wagons. *I guess I'll only keep one. I don't need any more. I don't need any extras*, he thought. And so it was with all his equipment. Whatever he had two of, he would sell one. The yard outside his barn was soon filled with all types of machinery and tools. Anything that he felt he no longer needed, he got ready to sell. Even the many rabbit hutches he and his sons had made were hauled out for the auction.

The auctioneer arrived that next morning to have George sign the contract. He was amazed when he saw all the machinery and equipment that he wanted to sell.

"You've got some pretty expensive equipment to sell, George. It looks like you've kept your machinery in good shape too. I hope, for your sake, there will be a lot of farmers here to buy what you're going to sell. I haven't seen any used equipment and machinery in better shape than what you have here."

"I've tried my best to keep my equipment in good shape, Leonard. I just hope the farmers like my cows as well. I've got some excellent milkers producing thirty to forty quarts a day."

The auctioneer had George sign the sales agreement and then went with him into the barn to look over his cows. George had twenty-five cows and five calves in the cow barn. Leonard was impressed with the size of the udders on most of the cows.

"It looks like you have some good stock, George. I'm really impressed. I'm sure the farmers who come to the auction will also be impressed. You've also kept them so clean even though they've been in the barn all winter!"

"I let them out in the barnyard every day for a an hour or so. It gives me time to clean out the barn and put down fresh bedding. I also keep them clipped so they don't get so dirty. You just have to know what to do, Leonard. Farming's not easy, but all you can do is the best you can."

"I'll have an ad put in the newspapers, George, advertising your auction. I'm sure once people know who it is that's having an auction, they'll come."

"Thanks, Leonard. My wife's a bit apprehensive. She doesn't think it's the right time to sell. But I can't do much farming anymore. The doctor says if I last a year, I'll be lucky."

"I'll do the best I can, George. The doctor may not really know either. It's good that you're quitting your dairy while the market for milk is good. It's a lot better than it was in the thirties."

George was given a copy of the auctioneer's contract. He only charged George 15 percent instead of the twenty he usually required. He felt confident the market was at a high point in the spring just before the cows are put out to pasture. *With the stock he has and the way he's kept up his equipment, George shouldn't have any trouble making a profit from the auction,* he thought.

It was a warm sunny day in late April. George and Marian had an early breakfast after George finished the milking that morning.

"Today's the day, Marian. The weather is just right for the auction. It's clear and sunny with the temperature around fifty degrees.

"I'm just glad Mom is no longer with us, George. She'd be heartbroken if she knew we were having an auction! This farm has been a dairy farm for more than three generations in my family. And now, it's all coming to an end!" Marian couldn't keep back her tears. "All these years! And now it's coming to an end," she said again.

"I know how you feel, Marian, but I can't do it anymore. Now that Kenneth isn't interested, we've got no other choice. I'm just glad he's still able to help me in the evenings and on weekends. I don't think I'm going to have the strength to do farming much longer. I feel worn-out just from milking the cows myself."

"You're right, George. We can't go on like this much longer. It's just so sad!"

The auction was scheduled for ten o'clock in the morning. The local farmers had already started arriving around nine o'clock. The first place they went was into the barn to look over the cows. Several of the younger men also climbed up the ladders on the silos and in the hay barn to look over as much of the inside of the buildings as they could. They also went through the machine shed and garage and looked at the machinery and tools that George had pulled outside the cow barn. There was nothing missed that they didn't look over ahead of time. Even the horse barn and horses were given a once-over.

On this Saturday morning, Kenny, together with the two men Leonard had working with him, brought out each cow on a rope to parade before the assembled farmers.

"Okay, gentlemen, who'd like to open the bid for this heavy milk producer at one hundred dollars? She gives more than forty quarts of milk a day. She's only five years old, and you couldn't ask for a better buy."

One man raised his hand. Another raised his at one hundred five. A third signaled the auctioneer. A fourth raised his hand, and one by one, the bidders only stopped bidding after one hundred twenty-five dollars was reached.

"Who'll give me one thirty?" the auctioneer chanted. After a couple of minutes of silence, the auctioneer said, "One hundred twenty-five once, twice. Sold to the man in the third row."

The auctioneer's assistant wrote down the name of each buyer and slapped a number on the cow's back that he recorded in his sales book. And thus, one by one, the cows were sold.

"You couldn't ask for a better herd of cows, gentlemen. George Murray has raised all of these cows from the time they were calves. They have an outstanding record of production."

By the time the sale of the cows had ended, the average had fallen to eighty-five dollars per cow. *Overall, not bad*, George thought. He had been to another auction, and the cows sold for less then eighty dollars per cow.

The sale of the machinery and tools was another matter. The silo filler sold for twenty-five dollars. The corn harvester for twenty. The old McCormack-Deering tractor sold for twenty dollars.

"You couldn't ask for a better tractor than this one," the auctioneer said. "George has had this tractor since 1914! It still runs perfectly, and he uses it for all of the belt jobs he needs on the farm!"

The farmers were impressed. But as one of them said, "If something breaks on it, who can repair it?" There was no answer.

His wagons sold for ten dollars a piece. His Model T pickup sold for just fifteen dollars. "Look," the auctioneer said, "this truck still runs and can still be used around the farm. You're getting a real bargain when you buy this truck!"

"Yeah, but you can get any parts for it anymore?" one young farmer questioned. "They don't make them anymore!"

"George never had a problem. If something was broken, he'd fix it! He knew how to repair whatever had to be used on the farm."

"Some of us aren't that smart, and we're too young to know how to fix an old truck like that!" one of the young farmers said.

The auctioneer had an understanding with George. Everything that was out in the yard was to be sold. Leonard was reluctant to let the truck go for such a low price.

"Where's George?" he asked his assistant. "I can't sell it for such a low price."

"Mr. Murray's gone over to his house, Mr. Cooke. He said he had to lie down a while. He wasn't feeling too well."

The auctioneer remembered George's instructions: everything that was out in the yard was to be sold. Reluctantly, he sold the Model T truck. By midafternoon, everything that was to be sold was sold. The buyers had arranged to have the cows shipped to their farms, if they didn't have a truck themselves. The tools and equipment would remain where they were sold until the buyer could hire a truck to haul them to his farm. Overall, George and Marian made roughly three thousand dollars of which four hundred fifty had to be paid to the auctioneer. George was satisfied with the result. It would now mean he didn't have to get up at four o'clock in the morning anymore to milk the cows!

G. When Generations Clash

Usually, the clash begins over some issue in which there is a difference of opinion between the adults in a family and a son or daughter over some issue in which youth attempts to change what has been the rule: you do what your father or mother tells you to do! It was really the first time I had ever quarreled with my father. He had always been the one whom I looked up to and listened to for his counsel and advice whenever he gave it. This time, it was different. I was twelve years old and increasingly conscious of what "other people thought." It was the spring of the year, and the grass was growing on our lawn, which ran across the entire length in front of our house along the road and down to the ditch going east to west.

"I'm going to tie the goats to the trees in front of the house and let them eat the grass. It'll save having to mow the lawn," he told Mom. "You won't have to mow it if they clean it up."

"What?" I asked. "You're going to tie the goats out in front of the house and let them eat the grass?"

"Yes. It'll save time having to mow it. They'll do a good job eating the grass, and it's already getting pretty high."

"You can't do that!" I said. "What will my friends think when they see the goats tied out on the lawn? I'll be embarrassed, Pop!"

"What do you mean, you'll be embarrassed? I can put the goats wherever I want! To hell with what someone else thinks!"

"But all of the kids on the school bus will make fun of me because of the goats being out on the lawn! They'll think we don't have a lawn mower!"

"I don't care what anyone else thinks! The goats are going to be tied out on the front lawn today!" Pop said even more emphatically. "If it embarrasses you, that's too bad, but the goats are going out on the lawn!"

When he spoke that way, I knew the conversation had ended. There was nothing more to be said. He would do what he wanted, not what his twelve-year-old son preferred!

It was just as I had predicted. My friends laughed when they saw our herd of goats tied to the trees eating the grass in front of the house.

"Hey, Fritz! Don't you have a lawn mower? We don't let our cows out on the lawn to eat the grass!"

The laughter and snide remarks continued. As more of the boys and girls got on the bus, the earlier pupils told them, "You should see what Fritz has on his front lawn! He's got some of his goats which they use as lawn mowers!"

They all laughed. There really wasn't much I could do about it. When the bus came back in the late afternoon, the goats were still there and remained for the rest of the week. After five days, the front lawn was completely mowed by the hungry goats. The embarrassment never really left me. I became increasingly sensitive to what other people thought. My attitudinal differences with my father increased over the years. I couldn't believe he would be so impervious to the opinions and views of others with whom we often had contact. His attitude was "I don't care what other people think! I'll do as I please!"

For a preteen, this started a long line of differences that increased over the years between what my father thought and did and my own views and actions. He was the product of another age, another culture, another set of experiences that I would never have. He grew up in an era in which what the head of the household said was law and beware of anyone attempting to challenge what he had learned to assume was the way things should be done. While I was more fortunate than my siblings in that he did not use corporal punishment on me, he did use it upon them if they should cross what he said or wanted to do. It was another reflection of the same pattern of behavior that his father had used: spank the earlier children, if they should challenge what he said, and spoil the last one. Pop only spanked me once for losing one of the wooden carvings from my brother's scoutmaster's exhibit. I had picked up a beautifully carved pistol to play with, and at the end of the day, I couldn't find it anywhere. I was eight years old at the time.

"You know what I said you weren't to take anything out of the box to play with, and now you've lost the little carved pistol. I'm going to have to spank you, Fritzle, for not listening to me. Come here!"

I came to him. He put me across his lap and gave me four good wallops across my bottom. I never did anything like that again!

It was four years later that I began to take exception to what he dictated. To his credit, he didn't exact corporal punishment upon me for not accepting what he took for granted I should accept. My differences of opinion gradually evolved through the years, and while our arguments often became heated, they did not result in physical abuse no matter how serious the differences were between us.

IV.

Growing Up

A. A Playground "Accident"

It was three-thirty, and we were all waiting for the school bus to take us home. Dale had brought a football to school that day, and he proposed we go out to the playground and play a pickup game. He and Bob chose up sides, and Dale kicked off to our team. After catching the ball, Bob ran with it until he was caught in the game of two-handed touch football about ten yards from the place where he had caught it. We huddled, and Bob suggested, "Fritz, why don't you go out for a pass. I'll throw it to you as soon as I see you're out in the clear."

We were playing football on the same field that was used for both softball and hardball practice by the Jayvee teams. The infield was bare and hard-packed dirt. It was almost like a sidewalk for its condition. Only in the outfield was there any grass, and even that was sketchy with intermittent hard-packed dirt. We lined up with our opponents across from us. Francis was lined up across from me. After Johnny centered the ball to Bob, I started running out to catch what I had thought would be a pass from Bob. As I ran past Francis, he stuck out his left foot to trip me. I fell down with a bang on the hardpack. I noticed, as I got up, my left arm did not respond to my attempt to bring it up to a level position. It hung down my left side and hurt. Dale said, "It must be out of joint. Here, let me pull on it to see if it snaps back into place."

He grabbed hold of it and pulled on my arm. Nothing happened except it hurt.

A FARM BOY SEES THE WORLD

"Let me try it again, Fritz," Dale said. Again, nothing happened, but it really began to hurt even more.

"Why don't you go over to the nurse's office and see what she can do, Fritz?" Dale suggested.

I walked over to the nurse's office and came in just as she was about to leave for the day. She saw there was something wrong right away.

"What happened to you, Donald? Why are you holding your left arm?" "We were playing football, Ms. Wager. Another boy tripped me as I went by, and I fell on my arm."

"Let me take a look at it."

She took me inside her examination room next to her office and had me take off my sweater. Since I could only get it over my head with my right arm, she helped me take it off over my left arm.

"Can you raise your arm at all, Donald?"

I tried my best but to no avail. "I can only raise it if I hold it with my right hand, Ms. Wager."

"Well, you've got to have a doctor look at it. I don't have an x-ray machine here in the office. Where do you live?"

"I live on the last farm in Onondaga County on Route 5."

"I'd better call your mother, Donald, and tell her to come and get you. You've really got to go see a doctor. It looks like it's broken."

"We don't have a telephone or a car, Ms. Wager. I ride the school bus back and forth. It's the only way I can get home after school."

"I'll take you home and talk with your parents. You live on a farm? Your father will be home too, won't he?"

"Yes. They're making hay today. My father and mother will be home." "Well, follow me out to my car, and I'll take you home. You've really got to see a doctor. It looks like you've got a broken arm."

I followed Ms. Wager out to her car behind the school. She opened the door for me to get in the front seat.

"Here, use this pillow under your arm." She took it out from the backseat and lifted my arm to place it on my lap.

"You live right on Route 5, Donald?"

"Yes. Our farm in the last one in Onondaga County?"

She didn't say much to me on the way to the farm. As we came closer to it, I said, "Here it is, Ms. Wager."

She drove into the yard and up to the back door of the house. Pop was on top of the hay wagon just putting the hay fork into the loose hay prior to getting off the wagon to drive the tractor attached to the hay rope and fork to draw the load into the roof of the barn. He then got off the tractor and came back to the wagon to trip the rope attached to the hay fork that drew the load into the hay barn. Mom was in the hayloft mowing the hay away from the dropping area to make sure there would be room for the subsequent hay fork loads coming into the hayloft. After Pop backed the tractor up to the barn, he got off and walked to Ms. Wager's car.

"Mr. Megnin," Ms. Wager began. "I think Donald has a broken arm or elbow.

He really needs to see a doctor."

Pop walked around to my side of the car and started in. "What were you doing to break your arm? How can we take you to a doctor when we don't even have a car? What were you doing playing football?" He cursed in German a few times. He told Ms. Wager, "I'll get my wife. She's in the hayloft. I can't leave the farm. I've got to milk the cows pretty soon!"

Pop walked over to the barn and called out, "Emmy. Kom runder. Donald hat seinen Arm gebrochen, und die Krankenschwester hat ihm vom Schul Heim gebracht." (Emmy. Come down. Donald has broken his arm, and the nurse has brought him home from school.)

Mom came down immediately ringing wet from sweat and particles of hay on her head scarf.

Ms. Wager introduced herself, "Hello, Mrs. Megnin. I'm Ms. Wager, the Fayetteville school nurse. Donald came into my office after school this afternoon because he has possibly broken his arm. He really needs to see a doctor and have it x-rayed."

"What?" Pop asked. "How can I pay for a doctor to look after him! I don't even have any money! You should have thought about that before you started to play football, Donald! It's going to cost me a lot of money! You shouldn't have been playing football!"

Mom looked in the window of the car where I was sitting. "I'll have to take him on the bus, Ms. Wager. The next one won't be coming by until five forty-five. I'll have to take him to the hospital by then because the doctor's office that we've used in Fayetteville will be closed."

"If you can go with us, Mrs. Megnin, I can take you to the Crouse-Irving hospital and have him examined by Dr. Potter. I know him, and I'm sure he'll be very helpful and understanding of your situation."

"Oh, thank you very much, Ms. Wager! I'll hurry and change as quickly s I can."

Pop stomped off to finish the unloading by himself. He didn't say anything to Ms. Wager. She was really doing him a big favor. Evidently, he didn't seem to feel it was necessary to say thank you. He was no doubt upset because of the cost involved with my broken arm.

Mom quickly changed her clothes after rinsing off her face and got in the backseat of Ms. Wager's car. Neither of them said much to each other or to me. It was a half-hour's ride to the city and hospital on Crouse Avenue. Upon arrival, Ms. Wager parked her car and accompanied us into the emergency room of the hospital. After seeing we were situated in the waiting room, Ms. Wager sought out Dr. Potter. She must have told him our family's limited economic circumstances. She no doubt told him she brought us to the hospital because we had no car. She must also have told him she would wait until he was through and take us back home again.

Dr. Potter was very pleasant man in his fifties, I would assume. His hair was turning slightly gray, and he had a graying mustache.

"Let's take an x-ray of your son's arm, Mrs. Megnin. He seems to be having trouble trying to lift it without using his other hand."

He placed me on a chair next to the x-ray machine and took a picture of my elbow. After scanning it, he came out and told Mom, "Your son has broken the bone at the tip of his elbow which makes it impossible for him to bend it. What I'll have to do is put a cast on it so that it's stationary for three weeks. It should be pretty well healed by then."

He placed my arm in a cast folded on my chest, which kept it in a firm diagonal position. When he had finished, he said, "That's it, Mrs. Megnin. Ms. Wager will take you home again. I'll expect you and your son to come here to the hospital in three weeks so I can see how he's doing. Is that okay with you?"

"Thank you very much, Dr. Potter. I don't know what we would have done without Ms. Wager and you. We really appreciate all you've done for my son."

"I'll see both of you in three weeks. In the meantime, make sure he keeps his arm dry."

Ms. Wager came back into the emergency room and thanked Dr. Potter for his services. "I can take you home now, Mrs. Megnin. Dr. Potter has taken care of your son's broken elbow."

We returned to the parking lot, and Ms. Wager drove us back to the farm. As we got out of the car, she reminded Mom, "Don't forget, Mrs. Megnin, Dr. Potter wants to see both of you three weeks from today."

"I won't forget, Ms. Wager. Thank you very much for taking us to the doctor and back home again."

"You're welcome, Mrs. Megnin. I've talked to Dr. Potter, and he understands money may be a problem for you in paying for Donald's broken arm. You'll be able to pay him in installments, if that's what you would prefer."

"Thank you. I'm sure my husband will be pleased that we don't have to pay for it all at once. We really don't have much money."

"I understand, Mrs. Megnin, and Dr. Potter does too. I wouldn't worry about it."

When the three weeks were up, Mom and I took the Syracuse-Utica bus and got off at the Crouse Avenue corner. It was a six-block walk up the hill to Crouse-Irving hospital. We went into the emergency room and waited a few minutes until Dr. Potter came out to take us into his examination room.

"How's the patient today?" he asked Mom. "He's doing fine, Dr. Potter."

"Do you have any pain, Donald?" he asked me.

"No. It hasn't hurt a bit."

"I'm going to take the cast off today, Mrs. Megnin. He'll have his arm in a sling for another couple of weeks. By then, you should be as good as new, Donald."

He cut off the cast and asked, "Can you bend your arm?"

I tried but almost fainted. He gave a gentle pull on it, and I seemed to black out. I almost fell off my chair.

"That's why you'd better wear a sling for another couple of weeks, Donald. When you come the next time, I'm going to really pull on your arm to make sure you can start bending it at the elbow again. You shouldn't have a problem after that."

"How much is this going to cost, Dr. Potter?" Mom asked.

"It won't be much, Mrs. Megnin. It'll probably be fifty dollars. I've talked with Ms. Wager, and I've agreed you can pay it in installments. Can you pay five dollars today?"

"Yes. My husband thought you would want at least a down payment on what you're doing for our son's arm."

"That's fine. If you're not able to pay it on a regular basis, don't worry about it. Pay it when you can."

"Thank you very much, Dr. Potter. We'll pay for it as soon as we can."

The next time Mom and I went to see Dr. Potter, he did, indeed, pull on my arm to try to bring it back to a level position as we sat across the table from each other. I almost passed out again. He let up pulling on my arm periodically just before I thought I was going to pass out. We did these attempts repeatedly for several minutes. Each time, I seemed able to hold out longer before feeling I was going to faint. By the time he was through stretching my arm, it almost reached the flat surface of the table from the ninety-degree position from which it started. After conducting these exercises, he said, "Keep doing these exercises, Donald. Have someone in your family pull on your arm until it reaches the flat surface of the table. Once you've reached that level, you shouldn't have to do it anymore."

Mom paid another ten dollars after that last visit and five dollars a month until the bill was paid off. Times were difficult in the nineteen thirties. Mom had to pay off her dental costs the same way: one dollar a week for two years!

B. Converting Words into Numbers

As a sixth grader, he felt when it came to numbers, he knew little or nothing about them. From first grade onward, he seemed to have a certain block when it came to adding them together. By second grade, he was astonished when the teacher said he and a little girl had scored perfectly on adding their numbers on the test she had given them in class. He couldn't believe it was possible, but his teacher said it was. By third and fourth grades, his apprehension had grown. It wasn't that he couldn't learn to add, subtract, multiply, and divide. He simply was afraid he was going to make a mistake using numbers in whatever version the teacher was presenting them. By the time he reached sixth grade, where arithmetic was to be used in "problem solving," he really felt stumped. He couldn't seem to translate words into numbers. When Mrs. Smith wrote problems on the board, which had to be converted into numbers, his fear of not knowing how to do so grew. She wrote several word problems on the board. His fear of translating the words grew even more acute! When he couldn't do the problems, Mrs. Smith suggested, "You'd better stay after school and work on learning how to solve problems in arithmetic."

The anxiety increased for fear he might miss his school bus ride home at four fifteen. *What would I do?* he asked himself. *How will I get home if I don't get on the school bus?*

Mrs. Smith gave him problems to solve after school, which he could never quite manage. When the classroom clock struck four, his restlessness grew.

"Mrs. Smith, my bus leaves in a few minutes. I can't finish these problems today."

What Mrs. Smith was not doing was taking him step by step through the procedure to learn to put the word's into arithmetical symbols that were used to present the problems to solve.

"Take the problems home with you," she told him. "Do them there and bring them with you tomorrow, and we'll go over them."

He was thankful the day had ended. He took the word problems home with him. *I'll get my brother to help me with this tonight,* he reassured himself. *He knows just about everything using numbers!*

"Could you help me after dinner?" he asked his brother. "I've got these three problems to solve in arithmetic. Mrs. Smith gave me words to put into numbers, and I don't know how to do that."

His brother was a high school senior. "Okay," he said after dinner. "Let's get started."

He spread the problems out before them. His brother said, "The problem asks, if the driver drives from New York to California in a week and the total distance is three thousand miles, how many miles does he drive in a day?"

"I don't know," his little brother said. "How do I change these words into numbers?"

"Okay," his brother asked, "how many miles is it from New York to California?"

"Three thousand," the little brother answered.

"Right. How many days did it take him to drive from New York to California?" his big brother asked.

"Seven," he answered.

"How do you know it's seven?" his big brother asked.

"It took him a week, and there are seven days in a week."

"Right. Now how do you determine how many miles a day he had to drive to get to California?" the big brother asked.

"That's just what I don't know! What do I do next?"

"Look, you know how many miles it is from New York to California.

Right?"

"Three thousand miles."

"How many days did it take him to drive out there?" "Seven."

"Okay. Now how many miles is it from New York to California?" "Three thousand miles."

"Okay. Now how do you know the number of miles he had to drive each day to go that distance?" the older brother asked.

"That's just what I don't know!" the little brother answered. "You know how many days it took him, right?"

"Seven days. I know that, but how do I find out how many miles a day he has to drive to get there in a week?"

"You've just said it!" his big brother replied somewhat angrily. "How many days are in a week?"

"Seven days."

"Look," the big brother said in exasperation, "if you know there are seven days in the week and it took him a week to drive out there, how many miles does he have to drive each day to get to California in a week?"

"How do I find out? That's just what I keep telling Mrs. Smith, I don't know!"

"You just said there are seven days in the week, right? The distance is three thousand miles, and he drives it in a week. How many miles a day did he drive to get there in a week? It's so simple, I can't imagine you don't know how to do it!"

"What do I do?" the little brother asked plaintively. "Do I divide the total number of days it took him to drive out to California?"

"Exactly! Now why was that so hard for you to understand?"

"I've always had a problem putting numbers to words! If It were simply numbers, I might not have trouble understanding what the problem is. But as soon as words are used instead of numbers, I get confused!"

"So how many miles a day must the man drive to reach California in a week?"

"Four hundred twenty-eight point six miles a day."

"Exactly! Here, let me do the rest of your problems. I've got some homework to do myself tonight. I can't spend all of my time helping you translate words into numbers!"

C. Equal Opportunity

Between the seventh green and the eighth tee is a delightful drive through the woods, swamp, and vines overhanging the cart path. The men liked to use this drive as a place to stop and relieve themselves before continuing their game of golf. The smell on hot summer days can be quite stifling. The aroma of urine mixed with the smell of a swamp can be somewhat overpowering to those who must frequent this passage to continue their progress on the golf course. Indeed, it had gotten so odoriferous that some of the lady members of the club protested to the board of directors to put a stop to this unseemly practice in order to keep the smell from upsetting anyone who happened to pass through that way. The Women Golfers Association had written a formal letter of protest to the board to take action on this gross misbehavior on the part of the Men's Golfers Association making it, they claimed, virtually unbearable for the ladies to drive their carts through this "stench-filled corridor through the woods"!

After receiving the letter, the board of directors listened as the president read the words from the Women Golfers Association and their request "We formally request that you prohibit the men from taking advantage of this otherwise beautiful pathway to urinate at their leisure while driving from the seventh green to the eighth tee. The odor is overwhelming and, therefore, should be prohibited!"

After considerable discussion and deliberation, the board of directors responded with the following statement:

> We wish to thank the members of the Women Golfers Association for bringing to our attention a real oversight on the part of the board of directors to the inequality of opportunity that has been placed upon them inadvertently. As of this day, the board of directors shall grant the members of the Women Golfers Association the same entitlement that has long been taken for granted as a rest stop between the seventh green and the eighth tee by members of the Men's Golfer Association.

Therefore, from this day forward and henceforth, this pathway shall be open to equal participation of the Women Golfers Association granting them the same privilege of a "rest stop" as that which has for so long been held exclusively by the members of the Men's Golfers Association.

D. And He Thought He Was the Father!

"Well," Carl told his wife, "this is the time of the year I have my yearly checkup. The doctor told me last year I was in excellent shape. Not bad for an eighty-year-old man, don't you think?"

His wife listened carefully to her husband of the last three years. She was thirty-nine, and he was now eighty. They had had a daughter that previous year during their second year of marriage. It came as a surprise to both of them. Jane (his wife) had been told by the doctor, "Your husband isn't very likely to be able to have sex much anymore at his age. Don't be surprised if he can't maintain an erection during intercourse. I'm sure he'll try, but don't be disappointed. He won't be able to perform as well as either you or he may wish."

Jane kept this information at the back of her mind. *I do have a friend next door*, she remembered, *who told me at our wedding, "If you're ever in need of sex, just let me know!"* And now, Carl was going for his yearly checkup again. The doctor checked his heart and pulse rate, did a CAT scan of his body, had him do some exercises sitting up in a prone position ten times. He had him stand on one foot and then the other to gauge his balance. He gave him a blood test for diabetes and cholesterol earlier before his appointment. After the exam, the doctor told him, "For a man your age, Carl, you're in excellent shape. How's your sex life with your new wife?"

"We don't do it as often as I might like, I suppose, but when we do it, there's still the old feeling of release! I guess it must be working fine. You probably don't know, but we had a daughter two years ago. Not bad for a seventy-eight-year-old man, is it?"

The doctor listened attentively. He wasn't sure how he should say it. Finally, he said, "Carl, you're a hunter, aren't you? Didn't you once tell me about a bear you shot that took you by surprise coming down the same trail you were on?"

"Yes. It was a great big grizzly bear. He must have weighed more than four hundred pounds!"

"You used a thirty-thirty Remington rifle, didn't you?" "Yeah, I had to fire two shots into him before he fell."

"Let me tell you the story of another patient of mine who was also a hunter. He wanted to go bear hunting one morning but was beginning to become somewhat forgetful. After getting all dressed up and ready to leave the hunting lodge, he went past the doorway and took his large umbrella with him thinking it was his rifle. As he was coming down the trail, a big grizzly bear was directly ahead of him. He raised what he thought was his rifle, and the bear fell dead right in front of him. Do you think he killed the grizzly with his umbrella?"

"No way! Somebody else must have shot the bear! He could never have done it with an umbrella!"

"I hate to give you this information, Carl, but you're like the hunter in the story. He couldn't have shot the bear with what he was using. The same thing might be said about your new daughter. You have to be able to perform in intercourse to have a baby. A man your age is like the hunter without a rifle! Unless you have the ability to perform, someone else did it for you!"

E. A Night to Remember

It was the night of our high school graduation. After the ceremonies were over and the awards, speeches, and recognitions were completed, a group of us thought it would be nice way to top off the evening if we went swimming in the Walsh Construction swimming hole near Minoa. The site was a huge former gravel pit that filled with water to a depth of more than seventy feet. It was rumored there was a steam shovel at the bottom that could not be saved because the water had so suddenly filled the excavation over a weekend. When the work stopped on Friday evening, by the time the workmen came back on Monday morning, it was completely filled with water! It took a couple of years before some of the local teens found it to be an excellent swimming hole on a hot day. If a person did not know how to swim, he or she was warned, "Don't even try it! It's way too deep, and there are no lifeguards on duty!" Hence, it was for swimmers only.

My brother, Volkmar, had given me the use of his jeep for the evening. Bill DuPree also had a jeep. Bob Ford, a Chevy sedan, Bob Vessey, a Chevrolet, and Tom Doxsee, a Dodge sedan. Pete Friederichs, Tom Doxsee, and Ned Mann had arranged for some of the girls from our graduation class to go with us with the understanding that it would be a night of "nude swimming." The girls simply asked, "We'd like to swim by ourselves, if you guys don't mind! You guys can go and do what you want, but we're going off by ourselves way up the beach from where you'll be swimming."

We boys swam in the nude at the south end of the east bank, and the girls swam on the north end. After swimming for a time, I got out of the water, dried myself off, and got dressed. The rest of the boys kept on swimming. Since I was dry and wanted to go to the Barbeque in DeWitt for a bite to eat, I turned on the jeep's lights. The cars were lined up facing the lake on the edge of the shoreline. Pete Friederichs had just come out of the water, followed by Doxsee and Ned.

"Turn off those dammed lights, Megnin!" They all submerged back into the lake, except for Pete. He was too far out to go back into the water! We heard the girls laugh. I turned off the lights and suggested it was time to go.

Reluctantly, the rest of our groups came out of the water (with the lights out), dried off, and got dressed. We drove to DeWitt for a hamburger and Coke before heading home from a memorable evening.

F. And the Neighbors Never Knew

The young couple had moved into the upstairs of the Welzners' house. Since it was on the second floor, the young couple thought there was no need to put up shades over the windows.

Nobody's going to climb up the hill and look into the window," Herb told his wife. "It's too steep. You'd have to get up to the field before you could look down into town anyways. We can save money not buying any shades. Our curtains are enough for the windows."

What Herb and his wife did not know was that the local boys often climbed the hill behind the house from which they could see the entire village. In fact, they could not only look over all the fields up the valley but could see almost to the Erie Canal! Actually, the local boys had often climbed the hill to wander over to the next houses in order to see if they could spot the pretty girls who lived there or were on vacation at their relative's house. If they climbed the hill on weekends, they were more likely to see the girls stretched out on blankets, enjoying the sun bathing over the summer. The hill, therefore, was a natural attraction for the boys of the village. It was just off the Gulf Road, and by going through the old village cemetery, they could climb the hill more quickly. If they went up the Gulf Road, it was longer. The shortcut proved to be a useful one for the boys when they wanted to mount the hill quickly.

Bob and Johnny liked to hike around the countryside. It was by chance they happened to pass the Welzners' house one evening from viewing the girls before returning for supper. As they looked down the hill, they saw Herb and his wife having intercourse. It was most unusual that time of day, they thought. They didn't know that the young couple had only recently got married, and Herb wanted to do it after he came home from work.

"Look what he's doing, Bob. He's doing it to her! Let's stay and watch a while before we go home," Johnny said.

Johnny and Bob were transfixed by the ring side seat they had found so close to where they lived. They watched and watched until Herb was finished. It didn't seem to take too long.

"He's fast," Johnny told Bob. "It takes me a lot longer to do it to my sister!"

Bob laughed. Johnny liked to talk about his exploits. He told Bob once that when he and his sister were going to do it for the first time, his dad overheard them talking and came into the bedroom. He said, "Here, let me show you how to do it, Johnny. There's nothing worse than a poor sex job! You've got to know how to do it right!" He then demonstrated how to have sex with his sister.

Bob and Johnny told some of the other boys in the neighborhood what they had discovered looking down from the hillside behind Welzners' house. "If you want to watch something funny, you should come with us tonight."

"Where are you going?" Harold asked.

"We're going up where we were last night. Herb and his wife do a quickie as soon as he gets home. It's really funny to watch."

"Have you taken your brother with you, Bob?" Harold asked. "No, he's still a little young for that."

And so, the three boys went as often as they could to the hilltop behind the house to watch the young couple have sex. Neither of the couple had a clue they were being watched night after night. It was the sport of young boys who learned from observation what married people do when they have the time.

V.

Ultimate Influences

A. A Premature Judgment

He called on a Monday morning. He talked with the cousin of his mother. "Inge, I think you better come over and see my mom this morning. We don't think she's going to last much longer. She sleeps all of the time. We've moved her bed downstairs into our dining room so that we can keep an eye on her. She wakes up occasionally and looks around, but she doesn't say much. If she lasts another day or two, I think it'll be remarkable."

"I'm sorry, Ray. We'll come over as soon as we can. Donald and Julie are here.

I'll tell them, and we'll come over together."

Inge called us and told us what Ray had said. "Why don't we all go together, Donald? That way, I can show you how to get to Ray's house. It sounds as though she's not going to live much longer."

"Okay, we'll be at your house in about twenty minutes."

Julie and I got in our car and drove down New Process Gear Drive and turned down Fly Road. We then turned on Kirkville Road and got on the interstate and drove to Route 690 that took us through Syracuse to Westvale where Inge lived. After we arrived, Inge said, "It sounds bad for Wally. Ray said she doesn't even seem to recognize him or Kathy. We'd better go right away."

Inge and Don got in her car, and he led the way to Liverpool. After about a fifteen-minute drive, we arrived at Ray and Kathy's. As we got out of the car, Ray looked down from the upstairs window and called out, "I'll be right down."

We waited at the front door, and he opened it shortly after we walked up the steps of his house.

"Hi, Ray, sorry to hear about your mother," I said.

"Hi, Donald and Julie. Nice that you could both come. Hi, Inge and Don."

We shook hands all around. Kathy greeted as we come into the front room. "It's good that you could come right away. I don't think Mom's going to last much longer. She seems incoherent much of the time. I have a hard time trying to understand what she's saying." Kathy led us into the dining room where Wally was in a hospital bed.

"Hi, Wally. How are you doing?" I asked as I shook her hand. There was no response. Julie, Inge, and Don did the same.

"She doesn't seem to even know we're here," Inge said.

"That's the way she's been for the last couple of days. She seems to go in and out of consciousness," Kathy told us.

"I don't think she even knows who we are," Ray told us.

"That's too bad, I would have liked to have said good-bye to her," Inge replied.

We spent the next half hour talking with Ray and Kathy. We kept looking over toward Wally's bed in case she would awaken. There was no response, however, during the time we were there. We finally said our good-byes, shaking Wally's hand even though she seemed unaware that we were doing so.

"It's really too bad, isn't it?" Inge asked. "I would have liked to talk to her for the last time. But she seems completely out of it."

We all shook Wally's hand and said good-bye to her. We then did the same with Kathy and Ray.

"We may see you sooner than we think," Inge told Ray as we were going out the front door. "The next time we see you, it'll be at her funeral."

"You can't be too sure of that," Julie reminded Inge. "She may snap out of it.

But if she's not eating, I suppose it may not be much longer." "Keep us in touch, Ray. Let us know how she's doing," I said. We shook hands with Ray and Kathy and left.

Since Wally's mom and husband, Ray, were buried at the Woodlawn cemetery just up from our family's grave sites, we stopped to look at our gravestones. I walked up the hill a little ways, and sure enough, there was a hole already dug in what was to be Wally's grave site. A blue tarp was spread over it to keep out the rain.

"Well, they're all set for her funeral," I told Julie when I came back to our car. "The hole's dug and covered at the present time by a tarp. I imagine Ray will wait before he has her name carved into the granite next to Ray Senior's grave."

"I'm sure he won't have that done until she has actually died," Julie said. "I'm surprised the grave has already been dug. Usually, that's done only after the person dies."

"Ray's just getting prepared, that's all. It is a little premature, but then, he won't have to wait long before she's buried," I commented.

After we visited Wally for what her son thought would be the last time, it was at the end of May. Before we returned to Florida in early October, we made one last trip to the Woodlawn cemetery. The hole was still there and still covered by the blue tarp. It remained that way for more than two years. At a recent visit to the cemetery, we saw that the hole had once again been covered with dirt (three years later). Wally had recovered and is now in an extended care community for retired persons. We not only have paid her visits but have played cards with her as well. The next time, perhaps, the grave site will be dug after her death and not before it!

B. The Importance of Words and Examples

It was on a Sunday afternoon in late June of 1946. The Reverend Alexander C. Carmichel spoke to our high school graduating class in the annual baccalaureate service. Our family contact with the church had been limited to the occasional attendance in the old Mycenae schoolhouse when the minister from the Kirkville Methodist Church came to preach and conduct the weekly service. Our neighbor, Mrs. Martha Spencer, took my mother and me along occasionally in her Chevrolet coupe. If we arrived early enough, I would attend the Sunday school class conducted by Burl Holtz in a little room off the main sanctuary. I found the topics that Burl used for discussions usually interesting. The class was mixture of all the youth from the nearby neighborhood ranging in age from grade school to junior high. Not having a car meant we were dependent upon Mrs. Spencer to take us whenever she felt so inclined. While Sunday school class was interesting, the service and sermons were beyond my comprehension. I sat in attendance because I had to wait for Mrs. Spencer to take us home again. No doubt, my mother and Mrs. Spencer seemed to like what they heard, but for me, it was simply time I had to sit through as quietly as possible. It wasn't until graduation from high school that I discovered religion could be more than esoteric phraseology and claims I could not understand with words that seemed to have no meaning to me as a boy.

Alex gave a sermon to us graduates that not only impressed me greatly but were words that I've never forgotten: "We must sacrifice our little tonights in order to experience our greater tomorrows!"

The thought of sacrifice and learning to forego current pleasures for the sake of greater future achievements was just what we teenagers needed to hear. It was to become a mantra that continually reminded me of the need for choices that I had to make.

"Don't forget," Alex said, "if you really want a future worth living, then you have to learn to make choices. It will not be easy. The choices you make will determine what kind of life you will have in the future! They will only be achieved if you weigh them very carefully and make your decisions accordingly. Only you can decide what you shall do and, hence, become!"

I had never heard someone say such words so clearly and precisely that could determine what kind of future a person could have. Not only was this experience an important bell ringer in helping me decide what I eventually would do, but it evoked a desire to hear more from Alex Carmichel. Bob Bolton, a high school classmate, was to become one of my best friends after high school. He encouraged me to come to the DeWitt Community Church. It was the one he and his family attended and invited me to come to one of the Sunday morning services. I did and was so impressed I started coming as often as possible. The sermons Alex preached resonated with me as nothing else had ever done. As time went on, Bob included me in his group of friends whom he took for visits to their summer camp on Otisco Lake. My work on the farm usually meant I had to be home by five o'clock on Sunday afternoons to help milk the cows. Fortunately for me, Mom and Pop often said, "Donald, if you want to go to the Boltons, go ahead. We'll do the milking ourselves this evening."

During the spring, summer, and fall, they allowed me to skip coming home on Sunday mornings after church. I had helped with the milking in the morning, and since we generally didn't work on the farm on Sundays, except for the evening milking, I had what I would call "free time" from nine to nine. (I tried to be in bed by then since I had to get up at four-fifteen each morning.) I began attending the DeWitt Community Church fairly regularly. Often, Bob invited me to come with him to his home for Sunday dinner.

Within two years of attending the church, Alex asked me if I might be interested in teaching a Sunday school class of eighth-grade boys prior to the Sunday services. I agreed. With the use of the Presbyterian Sunday school materials, I began to become acquainted with the theological underpinnings of Christianity. In retrospect, if I had not been so impressed with the sermons Alex gave each week, I probably wouldn't have continued adding to my list of things to do—preparing for the Sunday morning class. I was also taking the Henry George School of Economics home-study course during these days plus reading extensively in the books my folks received as members of the Great Books Club series each month.

Mr. and Mrs. Bolton, Bob's parents, often invited me to attend some of the Sunday evening functions at the church as their guest. Mr. Bolton was impressed with how many dates, persons, historical events I could recite whenever I was asked. Bob often said, "Geez, Meg, you really know a lot about history! My dad is really impressed with how much you know about current events!"

What Bob and his parents didn't know was the daily experience I had to discuss all sorts of issues, historical facts, and behavior with my father. While cleaning out the barn, milking, sawing wood, or driving back and forth in my jeep all over the farm, we had many discussions on all sorts of topics. It was not unusual for us to disagree completely on a given issue, especially after I started attending the DeWitt Community Church. Pop couldn't stand the preachers he heard on the radio to whom Mom listened occasionally on a Sunday morning. He also disliked and distrusted Alex. After our high school commencement, for example, he had seen Alex kiss one of the women parishioners of the DeWitt Church. From Pop's point of view, such an act represented a man who exploited women, if he didn't care about kissing one out in public! "You have to be careful with such a man, Donald!"

In retrospect, Pop's views were consistent with what he had learned as a boy and man growing up in the days of the German Empire. "A minister would never do that under any circumstances! You shook hands with your women parishioners, but you would never kiss them!"

Needless to say, I saw nothing wrong with this behavior on the part of Alex. I had observed him on a weekly basis in his interactions with all kinds of people who attended his church. I thought this was just the way Alex was. He treated everyone the same way. There were no favorites or obvious alignments with different persons. We were all the "sheep of his flock," as far as I could determine.

In the spring of 1948, Bob Bolton's dad had a heart attack from which he never recovered. Bob was devastated by his death. Those of us who were his friends were the pallbearers. It took Bob several months to regain his composure and gradually get over the trauma that his dad's death had caused him. Alex spent hours with him on a daily basis. He knew what Bob was going through. He had lost his own father at an early age, and it took him several years to come to terms with his death. Alex's example was another one of those "messages by illustration" that he employed so well as someone who cared what was happening to persons around him. As a consequence, Bob became aware of how important Alex was in helping persons overcome their grief from the tragedies that were also part of the experience of living. Alex demonstrated, by example, how to help people overcome whatever hardships might befall them. For those of us who were of post-high school age, Alex, together with Bob, set up what was known as the "College Club." Bob was attending university college (the night-school equivalent of Syracuse University) at the time, and since there were several teenagers in this category, all teenage boys and girls were invited to attend each Sunday evening. There was a group discussion of a topic that any member wished to have the group discuss. I also participated each week during the winter months, even though I was not in college. The group met from seven-thirty to eight-thirty each Sunday evening followed by a game of volleyball in the memorial hall. (Alex had persuaded the trustees and church members to build such a hall after World War II in order to meet the needs for a recreational center for the community's youth.) I had completed my work on the farm for the day by that time. While the club was open to anyone of the post-high school age even though not all of us were in college, it proved to be an excellent way for the members to become better acquainted with one another. We all looked forward to the weekly discussion. In the spring, summer, and fall, a number of picnics and softball games were held by the college club at county parks, Pratts Falls and Clark Reservation. It also proved to be an excellent way for the members to begin dating and even getting married, as time went on.

By the spring of 1950, after one of our Sunday evening discussions, Bob invited me to come to the apartment he and his mother shared in Syracuse. We had cake and ice cream for dessert. After which, Mrs. Bolton said, "Don, you don't know this, but my husband and I have been very impressed with you. He said he wanted to do something for you that would help you become whatever you wanted to be. We both felt you could become very helpful to people with their problems. We felt you should go to college and become whatever you wanted to be. We believe you should have an opportunity to study and use your talents to serve in whatever way you wish. My husband has left money for you to attend college whenever you can. The money is there for you to use."

Needless to say, I was overwhelmed! I almost couldn't fathom what she was saying.

"What Mom is saying, Meg, is that you should be going to college. You've got a lot to offer to people. All you need is to get an education."

"Talk it over with your parents, Don," Mrs. Bolton continued. "You don't have to make this decision right now. We just wanted you to know there's money for you to go to college full-time."

I thanked Mrs. Bolton and Bob. I drove home really elated with the opportunity, but it would mean a real change for my parents and me. I would no longer be able to work on the farm. It would mean a complete change for all of us. I told Pop and Mom what Mrs. Bolton had said that next morning at breakfast.

"Mrs. Bolton told me last night Mr. Bolton had left money in his will for me to go to college."

Both Mom and Pop stopped eating. "Wass? Er hat Dir Gelt gelassen so dass Du studiern kannst?" (What? He left money for you to go to college?) Mom asked.

Pop simply looked at me. He didn't say anything for some time. After I explained again what Mrs. Bolton had told me the night before, he listened very carefully and then asked, "Does that mean you can go to Syracuse University to study?"

"It does, but I'd have to be accepted first. As you know, I was turned down by them in 1946. This might make a difference. I don't think I could go anywhere else. I could probably continue on at university college, but I'd have to go full-time. What do you think I should do?"

"Donald, dass ist aber sehr Gut von Herr und Frau Bolton. Wann muestest Du anfangen?" Mom asked. (Donald that's very good of Mr. and Mrs. Bolton. When would you have to start?)

"What will this mean for the two of you, Pop and Mom? I couldn't very well continue on with farming and go to college full-time."

"Let us think it over, Donald. It's really too good an opportunity to miss since this is really what you've wanted to do." Both Mom and Pop agreed.

Over the next few days, neither of them said anything about what I should do. We were all taken aback by this opportunity.

"What would you like to study, Donald, if you went to college?" Mom asked me a couple of days later.

"From all of the reading I've been doing (Karl Menninger's, *Man Against Himself* most recently), probably psychology."

Mom didn't say anything at first. She said after a while, "That's an important subject that I also liked at the Froebel Frauen Seminar." (She had studied education and became a teacher during World War I in Germany.)

She and Pop must have talked this over because a few days later, Pop said, "Donald, I think you should go on to college and study psychology. That's an important subject and necessary in understanding human behavior."

"But if I go to college, Pop, I can't work on the farm at the same time!"

"You'll still be living at home, won't you?"

"Yes."

"Then during your vacation days and during the summer, you could help us on the farm. I'll buy your cows, tractor, and jeep. I can use them on the farm. We'll go to Syracuse and buy you a car. The jeep is too cold to drive during the winter without a heater."

Mom was very glad Pop had come to this decision. "I'm sure Donald will help us all he can, Papa. We can do the work during the year, and in the summer, he'll be a big help."

Not only did Pop buy my share of what I had invested on the farm, but we drove to the city a few weeks later, and he bought me a 1946 Ford coupe to drive back and forth to college. I was accepted at Syracuse University as a provisional student, which meant if I kept up my grades to a C level or better, I would be allowed to continue my education. Although I was never told, it was my suspicion that Alex had a hand in getting me into the university. He not only knew the chancellor but many of the administrative and teaching staff, several of whom were members of his church.

As I increased my time attending the DeWitt Community Church, I became increasingly interested in what Alex was doing. His influence affected me greatly. With the outbreak of the Korean War on June 25, 1950 and my attendance at Syracuse University in the fall, my status as an essential farm laborer no longer applied. Having been called up for a physical examination in the chimes building in downtown Syracuse as a prelude to being drafted into the army, Alex suggested, "There's no need for you to enter the army, Don. Betty and I will go with you to the draft board in Oneida this next week, and we'll plead your case for deferment."

Alex drove us to Oneida and, as he often did, wore his clerical collar. After introducing ourselves, the official whom we met was very gracious and noted what Alex said in my behalf.

"Don's going into the ministry, and I think he ought to have a preministerial deferment. He's been a farmer but has been given an opportunity to get his college education. Once he finishes college, he'll very likely go on to seminary."

"Thank you, Reverend," the official said. "I'll make a note of this in his file."

That very next week, I received notification from the draft board that I was granted a preministerial deferment. It was to be the start of working closely with Alex, Bill Cummins (the church administrator), and their staff at the church. I did visitations on prospective members and assisted, occasionally, in the Sunday morning services. After the haying season, I drove out to Indiana to attend the National Methodist Youth Convocation at Purdue. The following fall semester, Alex asked me if I'd like to join the staff on a part-time basis (twenty hours per week), to continue calling on prospective members. It was the beginning of an increasingly evolving network of jobs that I held on a part-time basis in the church until graduation from college. I was paid twenty dollars per week for my services, which by the third year included calling on parishioners in a few of the hospitals in Syracuse. Needless to say, Pop was not too pleased with this close association with Alex. He felt I was making a mistake in deciding to go into the ministry. One of the most devastating decisions for my parents, no doubt, as I think back on it, was my decision to join Bob Lindeman and Phil Resch to work with the forest service in Western Montana during the summer of 1952. It meant Mom and Pop had to do all the haying themselves! By my third year in college, Pop and Mom had given up farming. It was getting to be too much for them, and I was helping less and less each year.

Alex's influence became a demonstration for all of us who were going into the ministry not only of what he believed but also what he did. His example spoke even more loudly than his words at times. Before graduating from college in my senior year, I was asked if I would be willing to become the Syracuse in Asia representative from Syracuse University to Chulalongkorn University in Bangkok, Thailand for two years. In talking it over with Pop, Mom, and Alex, each of them thought it was a good idea. I'd see something of the world. Alex suggested I could ask for a postponement of my enrollment in seminary until I came back. I subsequently wrote to Dean Walter G. Muelder of the Boston University School of Theology asking to postpone my entry until I fulfilled my obligations to Syracuse University (two years in Thailand and one year on campus). He agreed I could postpone my entry into seminary following the completion of my obligations to Syracuse University. Upon completion of my overseas obligation, I was to work part-time in Hendricks Chapel on Dean Charles Noble's staff as the Syracuse in Asia representative. I was to give talks, show slides, and organize the annual money-making week of selling Asian products to raise money for the organization's support of my successor in Thailand. I was to begin my graduate work in psychology while working in this position at the chapel the same time.

On my way back from Thailand, I spent the summer not only visiting my relatives in Germany but also worked in an ecumenical work camp in West Berlin. During the course of this work, I became engaged to a German girl. When I returned to the States, one of my first stops was at the DeWitt Community Church to talk with Alex Carmichel. We spent more than an hour talking over what had transpired since I left two years previously. I told him of my engagement to a girl in Berlin and that she was coming to the States this next year.

"Don, if you're planning on getting married, you ought to have a regular job. You can't live on what you'll receive as a graduate student at Syracuse. Why don't you come and work with us this coming year? We've got plenty of work to do. (The church had built a new sanctuary and was expanding its membership to more than three thousand members.) We would hire you as an associate pastor for the year; then you could go on to seminary next year."

William F. Cummins, the business administrator for the community church and a close associate of Alex's, supported this idea.

"We could pay you four thousand eight hundred dollars for the year, Meg, and I'll even sell you my car for a good price!" (Bill had a fifty-five cream and blue Chevrolet sedan that he was willing to sell to me for two thousand dollars.) You know if you get married," Bill said, "it's going to cost you money."

"She's not here yet," I said. "She probably won't get a visa until this next year. Your offer does sound attractive," I told Alex and Bill. "I guess I better start saving money especially if we're going to seminary this next year."

"We'd love to have you on our staff, Meg. It would be great help to us and to you. Give it some thought and let us know as soon as you can," Alex suggested.

"Since you've put it that way, Alex, I guess I'll have to think over what to say to Dean Noble. That's where I was on my way when I stopped in to see you this morning. If I hadn't done so, it might have been a very different future for us. I'll talk with Dean Noble, but I'm already pretty sure of what I'm going to be doing this next year."

"Give him my best regards, Meg, when you see him this morning. Stop in on your way home and let us know what happened."

"Okay. I'll do that, Alex." We shook hands, and I drove up to the university. I parked behind the chapel. As I walked into the lower door on my way to Dean Noble's office, I stopped in the men's room. To our mutual surprise, there was Dean Noble next to whom I stood to urinate. We looked at each other and laughed.

"This is not the place I was expecting to meet you, Don."

"It isn't for me either," I said. "I was just on my way to your office. I wanted to tell you I've had an offer from Alex Carmichel that I really can't afford to turn down, Dean."

"What? You mean you're not going to be on my staff this year?"

"I'm afraid not. You see I've gotten engaged in Berlin this past summer, and we're planning on getting married this next year when she comes to Syracuse."

"Does that mean you're turning down your graduate fellowship in psychology?"

"Yes. I'm planning on going to the school of theology at Boston University in the fall of this next year at any rate. But I do plan to help with the Syracuse in Asia program as much as possible this coming year."

"Well, you can tell Alex Carmichel I don't appreciate him taking you away from us! I was counting on you to be part of my staff this coming year!"

After washing our hands, we shook hands. He asked, "Have you told Ruth Hoople yet about your change in plans?" (She was the director of the Syracuse in Asia program.)

"No, but I'll stop in and talk with her and tell her my change of plans."

We went our separate ways, and I stopped in Ruth's office. She was glad to see me.

"Thank you for sending us some of your slides, Don. We've had several programs these past two years showing them, and the students have been very interested in our program. Our Syracuse in Asia yearly sales have picked up nicely. We're looking forward to your participation in setting up programs for this next year. You probably don't know this, but we've selected your successor to Chulalongkorn University. He's Karl Schultz. Maybe you already know him? He left this past June to begin his teaching schedule for this year.

"Isn't he the one who was interested in getting a group together to go to India during the summer of 1953?"

"Yes, that's the one. You didn't get any funding as I recall, and your group never did go to India."

"That's right. He organized a series of lectures for interested students, but without funding, the program fell through. We learned a lot about India from the resource persons he scheduled."

"We're hoping he'll be as successful as you and Tom Gill were. We've gotten an excellent letter of commendation from the vice chancellor of Chulalongkorn University, thanking us for sending such good representatives from Syracuse University.

"I had a very good visit with him, Ruth, just before I left Thailand. He gave me an embossed silver cigarette case with my name on it as thanks for my service to Chulalongkorn University from 1954 to 1956."

"I'd like to see it, Don. I'm sure the students would like to see it too." "Ruth, I've just spoken to Dean Noble, and he wanted me to be sure I talked with you about this coming year. I've accepted an offer from Alex Carmichel, the minister of the DeWitt Community Church, to become a staff member at his church this current year. It'll mean I'm not going to be working here in the chapel. I'll be glad to help with your annual Syracuse in Asia Association sale, but since I'm getting married this next year, I thought it best to start saving some money. I'm going to forego my graduate fellowship in psychology and work full-time at the DeWitt Community Church."

Ruth was shocked. "You mean you're not going to be on our staff this coming year?"

"That's what I'm saying, Ruth. I'll be available for programs and to assist in your annual sale, but I'll be full-time at the community church."

"Well, tell me about your fiancée. Where is she from?"

"She lives in West Berlin. I met her at an ecumenical work camp repairing a neighborhood senior center in Neukölln, an industrial district in West Berlin. She is the secretary to the director of the center, and over the course of the summer, we got acquainted. We decided we should get married before I left Berlin. She won't be arriving here in the States until some time this next year. Since we're going on to seminary next year, I thought I'd better start saving some money to help cover our costs."

"Well, I certainly want to wish you both congratulations but we'll really miss you on our staff, Don. I can understand why you decided to serve on the church staff. It's probably a good decision for what you're planning to do. But for us, we'll have to get along with whatever assistance you can give us during the year. I was thinking of retiring one of these years. I guess I'll have to postpone that decision until a later time."

"I want to thank you, Ruth, for all you've done for me and for the Syracuse in Asia Program. Without your continued guidance and supervision of the organization, I don't think it would have been so successful. Using the Presbyterian Mission Board offices in New York and Bangkok is an excellent way to coordinate the services needed by those of us who are sent to Thailand. Without the contact of their field representatives in Bangkok, the administration of the monthly payment system, and the use of their doctors and health facilities, it would have been difficult for us to navigate in this foreign environment."

"Good luck, Don. We'll be calling on you to give programs and help with our annual sale in February."

We shook hands and I left.

And so the man who spoke the right words and exemplified what he was preaching by the demonstration of his life, Alexander C. Carmichel, became the model of the kind of minister I also wished to become.

C. The Man Who Made It Possible

Walter A. Bolton was the father of one of my best friends in high school and even more so in the post-high school years. Bob, the son of Walter A. and Doris H. Bolton, is the person who took me to the DeWitt Community Church for the first time. The Boltons were members of the church and not only attended regularly but sometimes invited me to join them for dinner in their Haddonfield Drive home in DeWitt. From the perspective of a farm boy, the Boltons were among the wealthiest people I knew. Mr. Bolton was the owner of a heat-treating plant in Syracuse. He was exceptionally friendly and laughed easily at the stories he heard from not only his friends but even from the occasional visitor (me) when I was invited for dinner. Mr. Bolton once waxed eloquently about how much he enjoyed the ham dinner Mrs. Bolton had made for us on that Sunday. I said, "I'm not too fond of ham, Mr. Bolton. I'm sure it was good. It's simply not what I prefer to eat."

He laughed uproariously at my comment. "That's what I like about you, Don. You're honest and straightforward. You tell the truth as you see it! Not enough people do that these days!"

He enjoyed telling this story over and over to their friends, from what Bob told me. "Dad was always impressed how you said what you thought. There weren't enough people doing that as far as my dad was concerned."

Mr. Bolton was the man who made my college education possible. He and Mrs. Bolton not only took Bob and me with them when they went to a concert or a play but they didn't seem to mind when I spent time visiting Bob in their home. It was a unique opportunity for me to get to know the Boltons and to spend what I would now label "quality time" with them. Unfortunately, Mr. Bolton died within two years after I had gotten to know him in 1946. It was truly an enormous loss for Bob, his mother, and all of us who knew him. It was a reminder of how short life could be when you most expect it to continue for years to come. Mr. Bolton fulfilled the adage as "one of the most unforgettable persons whom I have ever met." As brief as the time was that I knew him, he left an indelible imprint upon my life that changed the course of it in its entirety. It was his legacy that provided me with the funds to attend college and go on to attempt to do in the field of education what Alex Carmichel had done in the ministry.

D. Words of Wisdom

As people grow older, you would think they would become increasingly skeptical about what they hear, see, and assume. One would think what has been conveyed to them throughout history is nothing more than the assumptions and prejudices of those who occupied positions of authority in their given society. When the priest says, "In the name of the Father and of the Son and of the Holy Ghost," all members of his flock are expected to genuflect and repeat the words as if their recital will make them feel closer to their faith and the founder of it! When the minister repeats the words, our Heavenly Father, the congregation is supposed to think and feel whatever it is that has begun the events of the world must truly be a father figure reflecting the millions of years of control that the males have exercised over women and children by virtue of physical strength. There are relatively few persons who question these assumptions that cannot be proven and are purely a reflection of years of indoctrination, custom, tradition, and expectations passed from one generation to the next. What is so hard to understand for those of us who believe it is necessary to test and confirm what has been stated is the difficulty we have with well-educated adults who do not refuse to let scoundrels dictate what they should or should not believe: that such persons should allow themselves to be convinced that the mythologies of religion are to be viewed as scientific facts and the true experiences in the lives of grown men and women! From a psychological point of view, the belief systems proclaimed by human beings seem to have progressed relatively slowly and illogically in the context of modern science and technology that surrounds so much of our lives in our modern, advanced nation-states. Is this a reflection upon the dichotomy that still exists between what is known and what is part of the unknown that seems to confound human beings from generation to generation? If a person were asked what he or she believed about what happens upon the death of someone, there would very likely be all kinds of responses depending upon the background, experience, belief system, and indoctrination that he or she has had during the course of their lifetimes. Few, if any, would say, "I don't know. I'll wait until I get there or experience death myself." Such a response would be most appropriate, but how seldom this point of view is conveyed! We fall back upon the beliefs, prejudices, preferences, and "what we have been told by our clergymen, rabbis, swamis, imams, or monks whom we respect for their judgment or erudition" to believe what they have taught us to believe. Hence, prejudices, fallacies, radicalism, extremism, and nonprovable beliefs go with the departed.

Some thinkers have categorized religion as "the opiate of the people" because they believe human experience has to be tested to prove its truth or falsity. While many critics of religion are intolerant of those who disagreed with them, their concept of proof as the test of belief is one that we seem to have overlooked. A belief system that cannot be proven is, therefore, nothing more than a figment of a person's imagination, hope, expectation, or wishful thinking.

I would submit, what should be guiding a person's life is to ask himself or herself, "How can I best achieve the maximization of the talents I have as a productive, contributing member of the culture and society into which I have been born?" My relationship with my fellow human beings is the most important that I shall ever have. Therefore, I should be the one who respects their right to believe and do what they prefer so long as it does not infringe upon my right to do the same. The difficulty with this concept, however, is that as persons gather into groups, congregations, or specialized (religious) societies, the individual is not longer able to think for himself or herself. He or she has to adjust to the norms of the community of which each is a part even when such conformity conflicts with his or her own beliefs, practices, or traditions. There seems to be no room for individualism or the countenance of differences if they conflict with the majority's preferences or point of view should such a person reside in an intolerant community.

And such are the words and thoughts of one who has moved from accepting these traditional belief systems to questioning what is real and unreal, true or false, verifiable, or nonverifiable in repeated tests that can be conducted by anyone to his or her own satisfaction. Belief is ultimately a matter of choice that may or may not be rational, testable, or repeatable in the laboratory of human experience. For some of us, this is why we are no longer willing to accept the "teachings of various religious communities" even among those in which we've "grown up." In so far as the ultimate end is concerned, "we won't know until we get there," and very likely when we get there, we will have lost the capacity to differentiate between fact and fiction at any rate!

www.ingramcontent.com/pod-product-compliance
Lightning Source LLC
LaVergne TN
LVHW040149080526
838202LV00042B/3090